Caught in the Undertow

Undertow

(Sydney and Coen)

ISBN-13: 978-1497369160

ISBN-10: 1497369169

Caught in the Undertow

Book Six of the Hawaiian
Crush Series

E. L. Todd

"Sydney, where did you put the data sheets?" Dr. Goldstein asked.

Sydney appeared from behind the aisles. "It's in the raw data binder, Dr. Goldstein."

He shook his head. "Call me Gilbert, honey. We're family now."

"Oh yeah…old habits die hard," she said with a laugh.

Gilbert opened the binder and flipped through the pages. "I found it."

"Phew," she said. "I was pretty certain I kept it in there."

"Could you make sure all the glassware is cleaned before you go?" he asked while he made notes in the binder.

"Already did," she said with a smile.

"Well, I need this data made into a spreadsheet along with a few charts."

She walked to him and extended the document. "Already completed."

He looked at her, amazement in his eyes. "Syd, I can't keep up with you."

Her cheeks blushed. "I always give my best effort."

Gilbert shook his head. "I'm not sure what you see in my nephew. His brains are the size of breadcrumbs compared to yours."

She laughed. "He's very smart—just not as motivated."

"Yeah, that's what it is," he said sarcastically. "I guess he's smart for marrying you. I'll give him that."

She blushed again.

"How's the married life?" he asked while he restacked the binder. "Do you want to kill him yet? I wouldn't judge you if you divorced him."

Sydney laughed. "We're very happy."

"If you need me to smack him around, just let me know."

"Don't worry. I keep him in line."

He laughed. "I'm very glad you're my research assistant. Normally, I take on a Ph.D. candidate, but I have to admit, you're much better. I don't think I've ever worked with someone who was so intelligent."

Sydney averted her gaze and clenched her hands together, feeling more pride than ever before. "I'm glad you like having me here."

"Glad?" He laughed. "I love having you here."

"Working with you has been a dream. I think I have a good chance of getting into a Ph.D. program because of this experience."

He smiled at her. "Honey, you had a good chance anyway. Where do you want to go?"

"Well, I would prefer to stay here. Coen has his job and he may finish a semester after me."

He nodded. "The university in Monterey, California has a fine program. The trenches along the coast are the deepest on the planet. They are buzzing with undiscovered life. And you couldn't go wrong with the barrier reef by Australia."

Sydney's eyed widened. "I would love that. But I'm married and I have to think of Coen."

He shook his head. "Who cares about that knucklehead."

Sydney looked at him. "It sounds like you don't even like him."

"I hate him."

Sydney laughed.

"Nah. I love that kid to death. He and Jordan are the sons I never had. I'm very happy that he found you, Syd. I'm not totally ignorant to Coen's actions. I know he used to have a lifestyle very different than the one he has today. I'm glad you straightened him out."

Sydney didn't know what to say to that. It was an awkward topic.

"I'm headed to Vivian's for dinner. Would you like to join?"

"Sure," she said. "I love her cooking."

He put aside his binders and locked up the room. Sydney followed behind him with her bag over her shoulder. When she got outside, she looked down the dark hallway. Memories of her time working as a janitor came to her mind. She, Henry, and Nancy used to have so much fun being together, picking up the penguin poop and cleaning the windows. Now they all went their separate ways. Nancy was an artist, Henry was a writer, and she was a researcher. Everything worked out.

She walked to her jeep in the parking lot, and Gilbert made sure she got inside before he started his car. They drove to Vivian's house and parked outside. When they walked through the door, Sydney's mother-in-law jumped up and down.

"What a wonderful surprise," she said as she hugged Sydney. "Hello, dear."

"Hey, Vivian."

She pulled away and looked at Sydney. "It's Mom."

Sydney smiled. "Sorry, Mom."

Vivian gave her a warm smile and patted her on the back. "We're just about to eat dinner."

Jordan came down the hall and hugged Sydney. "Hey, what are you doing here?"

"Uncle Gilbert invited me."

"What about Coen?"

"Oh," Sydney said. "I forgot to call him."

Jordan nodded. "This is even better. Coen's annoying anyway."

Sydney laughed. "Well, that was sweet."

He shrugged. "Whatever."

They went to the dinner table and sat down.

Coen's dad smiled at her. "Hey, glad you could join us. I prefer you over Coen anyway."

"That makes two us," Gilbert said as he dug into his food.

Sydney laughed, knowing they were just joking.

"How was work?" Vivian asked Gilbert.

Gilbert wiped his mouth. "It's a little embarrassing when you realize your apprentice is a lot smarter than you."

Sydney felt her cheeks turn bright red.

"After my first biology exam, I dropped out of the class," Jordan said, shoveling food into his mouth. "I knew it wasn't for me."

"If Coen can do it, so can you," Vivian said.

Jordan laughed. "You got a point."

"What are you majoring in now?" Sydney asked.

"Business," Jordan said. "I'm going to go into construction like my dad, expand the empire."

Nathan rolled his eyes. "He's money hungry."

"Money, what's it like to have that?" Gilbert asked with a laugh. He looked at Sydney. "I'm glad Sydney is in this profession because of the passion, not the income. She won't be making anything."

Sydney ate a piece of bread. "As long as I have that shack, I'll be fine."

"And Coen will take care of her," Nathan said. "I know I raised my son right."

Sydney smiled. "He does a very good job." She ate her asparagus and another roll, loving the fact that no one berated her for being a vegetarian. She was usually teased for it by people she met, but none of them ever commented on it.

"Is my son being a good man?" Vivian asked.

"When he picks up his dirty socks and cleans up after himself," Sydney said with a laugh.

4

Vivian smiled. "I'm glad you put him in his place, dear. He needs a woman like that."

"He's very sweet," Sydney said. "The other day, he made me dinner. Well, he tried."

Nathan laughed. "I hope you like burned food."

Sydney shrugged. "It was the thought that counted."

"What did you end up eating?" Jordan asked.

"We got tacos instead," Sydney said.

Vivian shook her head. "Nathan could never cook either. Now we have a policy; only I'm allowed in the kitchen."

"Well, I can build a house," Nathan said. "That's a lot harder than cooking."

Gilbert rolled his eyes. "True love at its finest."

Sydney laughed at his jab.

Jordan turned toward her. "Hey, do you have any single friends yet?"

"None that are young enough for you."

"Any new janitors at the aquarium?"

She shook her head. "Sorry."

"Bummer."

"You're so young anyway," she said. "There's no rush."

"I don't want to get married," he said quickly. "I just want to meet girls." He winked at her.

"It's like Coen all over again," Sydney said.

"I hope my second son grows out of it as well," Vivian said.

"Don't count on it, Mom."

Sydney finished her plate then sat quietly while everyone else finished. She didn't feel awkward spending time with Coen's family without him. She felt welcomed and appreciated among them, like she was one of them.

When they moved into the living room to watch TV, Sydney headed to the door. "I should get home."

"That's right," Vivian said. "Coen is probably starving."

"He's fine," Nathan said. "He's probably eating a burned frozen dinner."

Sydney laughed. "Good night."

Vivian hugged her. "Love you, honey."

"I love you too."

Vivian pulled away and smiled at her.

"I get one too," Nathan said. He hugged her tightly. "Come over more often—without Coen."

"And bring a friend!" Jordan shouted.

Sydney laughed again. "I'll see you later." She got inside her Jeep then drove back to the shack. When she pulled up to the house, she saw the lights shine through the window. She stayed at his parents' house longer than she meant to. It was already late.

She walked inside then saw Coen sitting at the kitchen table. He stood up when he saw her, wearing a t-shirt and shorts.

"I was just about to call you," he said as he approached her.

"I'm sorry I'm home so late."

He cupped her face then pulled her hair back. "How was your day?"

"Good. How was yours?"

"Shitty until you came home." He pressed his face close to hers then wrapped his arms around her. His breaths fell on her skin, warm and heavy. Even though they'd been married for months, the heat between them never died. The heat always burned between her legs when she was alone with him. She could feel the same tension emit from him.

Coen pulled her to his chest then moved his hands up her shirt, feeling the skin of her waist. "What took you so long?" he whispered.

"Your uncle and I were working late then we went to your parents' house for dinner."

"Without me?" he asked incredulously.

"I forgot to call you."

He sighed. "I knew this would happen."

"What?"

"My family likes you more than they like me."

She shrugged.

"Those assholes," he said with a smile. "But I can't hold it against them. But an invite would have been nice."

She smiled. "I'm sorry."

"Your husband has been hungry all night."

"I know my husband can feed himself. He's a caveman, but he knows how to do a few things."

"I didn't mean I was hungry for food." The meaning of his words fell heavily on her ears. When he moved his hips against her, she felt his erection pressed against her stomach. Sydney had homework to do and needed to get ready for school in the morning, but now she forgot about it.

Coen moved his hands under shirt then felt her bra, squeezing it with his large hands. Her breathing hitched as she felt him. Every time they made love, it felt like the first time. Coen rubbed his nose against hers as his hands unclasped the bra, allowing his hands to grip her bare tits. He loved her breasts, loved touching them and kissing them. He didn't know what he liked more, her chest or her ass. Coen squeezed her then rubbed his thumbs over the nipples. Sydney felt her heart race as her husband touched her.

Coen pulled her shirt off then removed her bra. She stood in just her shorts, her top bare. Coen stared at her flat stomach, feeling the soft skin with his hands. Her abdominal muscles were prevalent, strong and noticeable. He loved the strength of her body. She wasn't weak and limber. She was powerful and beautiful like a real woman. She was his ideal fantasy, someone that was just as beautiful on the inside as well as the outside. He kneeled and kissed her stomach, worshipping his wife and the ground she walked on. She was his queen, his goddess, and he never grew tired of praising her.

Sydney watched him, her fingers running through his hair.

Coen stood up then kissed her breasts, sucking each nipple. He loved the taste of her skin, always so sweet and delicious. His hands gripped her waist, holding her steady. When they were home in the evenings, she belonged to him exclusively. He dominated her, fulfilled all of his fantasies. He came back up then cupped her cheek, staring into her eyes. When he saw the desire and love burn in them, he knew she was wet down below. He brushed his lips against hers, making her moan quietly, waiting for him to kiss her. Coen loved teasing her. He leaned in and kissed her lips, feeling the burn on his mouth.

Sydney breathed into him, panting because she wanted more. Coen always touched her in just the right way, made her more excited than she ever felt. She never grew tired of being with him. After they got married, she wondered if the sex would die. If it would grow cold and repetitive. Somehow it got hotter, sexier. She was glad they didn't have any neighbors, otherwise they would have gotten a lot of complaints by now.

Sydney grabbed his shirt and pulled it off, revealing the chest and stomach she loved so much. Coen continued his job as a personal trainer and his body was toned and fine just as it was before. She loved running her hands down, feeling the grooves and mounds of muscle. Her breathing increased the longer she felt him and kissed him. Somehow he made her crumble. She was on the verge of coming from the act alone.

Coen picked her up, kissing her the entire way, and led her into their bedroom. They replaced Sydney's small bed and got a king size mattress, large enough for them to roll around on. He placed her at the edge of the bed then grabbed her legs, unbuttoning her jeans. Sydney was so hot for him that she kicked them off quickly.

Coen smiled when he saw her enthusiasm. "You miss me, baby?"

"Hmmm…"

He moved on top of her, his fingers gripping the fabric of her thong. She received a lot of lingerie for her bridal shower and Coen loved seeing her wear them all. He'd never seen anything so sexy in his life. He pulled them off slowly, making her whimper in anticipation.

Sydney grabbed his shorts and boxers and pulled them off, his cock popping out. She moaned when she saw it, grabbing it by the shaft. She loved how big and thick he was. His size always hit her the right way. When they first made love, she didn't think she could handle him. Now she took him like a pro every time.

Coen leaned over her and pulled her further up the bed. He looked down at her while he held himself over her. She spread her legs, wrapping them around his waist. She wanted to feel him so much, she thought she would scream. If she didn't make love to her husband, she went crazy. She needed it every single day otherwise her routine was off. The morning sex and evening sex were a ritual.

Coen kissed her gently, feeling her tongue against his. Her lips were still gaping open when he pulled away, moving down to her hip. He kissed the tattoo, his tongue moving across the blue seahorse. It symbolized him, making her belong to him forever. Even when he couldn't see it under her clothes, the memory of it made him hot. He never thought tattoos were particularly sexy, but it was the hottest thing in the fucking world to him. Sydney was such a good girl, always following the rules. The fact that she broke one of them for him made him tremble.

Sydney gripped his hair while he kissed her hip, treasuring the tattoo she got for him. It was hidden from the entire world under her clothes, making it exclusively his when they were alone. Their sexual relationship had escalated even higher since she got it. Coen finished then came back to her, his heavy cock leaning against her stomach. She wanted to feel him inside of her so much, she'd beg if she had to. His cock was nirvana for her. She grabbed his forearm then brought it to her lips, kissing the tattoo of the green seahorse he had. The image was large, taking up his whole forearm, and she loved seeing it on him. It was the way he saw her, his life partner, and he wanted the whole world to know who his mate for life was. It was the sweetest gesture he ever made. He didn't even tell her he was doing it. Coen just came home with it on his arm. Coen watched her kiss his skin, seeing the love and adoration in her eyes.

He pulled his arm away then moved further over her, separating her legs. She breathed a sigh of pleasure, happy that she was finally going to feel him. Coen felt his dick twitch at the sight. Seeing the need in his wife's eyes was the hottest thing he'd ever seen. She was silently begging him, pulling his waist toward her. He thought he was obsessed with sex but Sydney was a million times worse than he was. If she didn't get her daily dose of morning and evening sex, she was moody.

"Coen, come on…"

"You want me to make love to you?"

"Please," she begged. She ran her fingers through his hair then pressed her breasts against his chest, rocking against him gently. "I'll beg, I'll plead," she whispered.

His cock twitched again. "My wife never has to beg me."

"Then stop making me wait."

He pressed his head inside her, stretching her slightly.

Sydney was already moaning, loving the feel of him.

Coen moved in slowly, taking his time as he moved all the way inside.

"God yes!"

He rocked into her gently, pressing his face close to hers. When he stared into her eyes, he saw everything that he loved about the world. She made him feel whole and complete, repaired after all the damage that happened to him. He never thought falling in love would fix all his problems. And being married was the best thing that ever happened to him. Somehow he wanted her more, found her even more attractive, and felt his heart hurt every time he looked at her. He was happier than he ever thought he could.

Sydney gripped his shoulders as she felt him move inside her. Every thrust felt right, hitting her in just the right way. Her husband knew her body better than she did. He always knew what she liked, when to push her, and what sent her over the edge. She spread her legs wider apart, wanting it harder and faster. Coen delivered, rocking into her from above. She dug her nails into his skin, enjoying everything he was doing to her body. The orgasm started as soon as he entered her, just as it always did. When she felt it burn between her legs, Coen pressed his hand against her clitoris and rubbing her aggressively, making her skin burn in euphoria.

"Coen...Coen."

He kept up the pace. His hands pinned back her legs and he thrust into her with even strokes, pushing himself all the way inside until he pulled out. She was wet like she always was, giving just the right amount of friction for him to enjoy their lovemaking. When he stared down at her, he saw her face flush red. Her nipples hardened. The feel of her insides was so good, so smooth. He was always caught off guard by how good it felt. He knew it was because he was madly in love with Sydney, the heart and soul of his world.

Sydney gripped his forearms. "Don't stop."

"You know I always make you come hard."

"I'm almost there…"

He pressed his lips against her, kissing her gently. "I love you, seahorse."

"Oh…yeah."

Coen stared at her, fascinated by the sight. He loved watching her cum. It was the best porn he'd ever seen. When he watched her mouth gape open and her eyes shine bright, he felt his body tense then relax as he came inside her. Knowing he was releasing a part of him within her always made the orgasm a million times better. He moved into her harder and faster, wanting to release as much as he could. "Baby…"

She rolled her head back and caught her breath. "That was good."

"Thank you. I aim to please."

Sydney ran her hands down his chest, lightly touching him.

"I love watching you come."

"Me too."

He leaned down and kissed her neck, licking the sweat from her skin. "I love you, wifey."

She smiled. "I love you too, hubby."

"I'm so glad my wife has such a nice body."

She rolled her eyes. "And has a great personality."

"Yeah whatever," he said with a smile. "Now let's get to bed."

"I need to study and take care of a few things."

"No."

"No?"

"You heard me. And I don't have an accent so you understood me."

"Coen—"

"You go to school and work all day. When you come home to me, you're mine. Everything else can wait."

She stared at him. "I have responsibilities."

"And spending time with your husband is important, if not the most important one."

Sydney sighed. "I'm sorry. I really don't mean to be a workaholic."

"I know you're passionate about what you do. That's fine with me. But I want to have dinner with you at night, watch TV, and hold you. The time we have together is precious to me. I don't expect you to spend all your time with me, but I better get at least two hours."

"Okay," she said quietly.

"Now let's go to bed. Unless you have an exam in the morning, it can wait."

She pulled back the covers and snuggled under the sheets. Coen came beside her and wrapped her in his arms. His large body acted as a natural heater, warming up the sheets and the enclosed space. Coen rested his face close to hers, his lips near her ear. He stared at her for a while before he closed his eyes.

"Goodnight, baby."

"You're amazing in bed," she mumbled.

He chuckled lightly. "Because you make it easy."

She mumbled again but he couldn't decipher her incoherent rambling. He fell asleep a few moments later, his wife held in his arms.

2

When Sydney walked into the cafeteria, she saw Ren and Henry sitting at their table.

"Hey," she said as she sat down.

"Where's your other half?" Henry asked.

Sydney shrugged. "He's probably talking to a professor."

"Do you guys have a class together?" Ren asked.

"We have molecular biology."

Henry cringed. "I bet Coen is cheating off you."

Sydney laughed. "He wishes."

Henry laughed. "Just because he's married to you doesn't mean he gets the hookup."

"Coen is actually very smart, smarter than me," Sydney said.

Henry rolled his eyes. "Sure…"

"I'm being serious," Sydney said. "I spend hours studying the material. He sits in class once and just gets it. I'm so jealous."

"Why?" Henry said. "You study the material so you'll know it forever. He probably forgets everything in a few semesters."

Sydney shook her head. "I know Coen acts like a stupid caveman that doesn't know his nose from his ass, but he's really smart. That asshole personality blocks it out."

"I can't tell if that's a compliment or not," Coen said from behind her. "It was masked with a lot of insults."

Sydney turned around, giving him her brightest smile. "It was meant to be a compliment."

His eyes narrowed at her. "I'm sure…" He sat down and put her lunch in front of her, a Caesar salad with no chicken.

Ren smiled. "That's sweet. You still bring her lunch even though you're married."

"Why would it change?" Coen asked.

"Well, you got the girl. You don't need to keep up the act," Ren said.

"I still want sex," Coen said. "You have to put a quarter in the vending machine to get a candy bar."

Sydney eyed him. "Are you comparing me to a *vending machine*?"

Coen laughed. "It's a metaphor."

"It wasn't very romantic," Sydney said.

"Well, we don't always make love. Sometimes we just fuck like animals."

Sydney rolled her eyes. "Okay. That's enough. I don't want Henry and Ren to throw up."

"If they haven't already, we're good."

Sydney turned back to Henry. "How's school?"

"It's good," he said. "I got a compliment on my paper from the president of the university."

"Cool," Sydney said. "What was it about?"

"How students can lower the cost of college with a few tips," Henry explained. "And I love writing. I'll never pick up penguin poop again."

"What's wrong with penguin poop?" Andre asked as he approached the table.

Henry smiled. "You and both know we hate those assholes."

Andre sat down and opened his sandwich. "Those birds are my arch nemeses. I'll be the victor in this battle."

"What battle?" Sydney asked. "I never had any problems with them."

"You didn't?" Henry asked.

"No," Sydney said. "They were really sweet. They would eat the fish out of my hands."

Henry and Andre both glared at her.

"What?" she asked.

"Forget it," Henry said.

Derek and Paola approached the table.

Derek pulled out the chair for her then kissed her on the forehead. "What would you like, baby?"

"You really don't have—"

Derek was gone.

Sydney looked at Paola. "In my experience, just tell him what you want."

"But you're married," Paola said. "You have the same bank account."

Sydney shook her head. "Coen was the same way before we got married."

Coen put his arm around her chair. "I have to make sure my lady is well fed. I like her muscles."

Paola smiled. "You guys are so cute."

"You should have heard them argue a second ago," Henry said.

"We fight sometimes, but we always make up," Sydney said.

"I kinda want to fight right now," Coen said with a twinkle in his eyes.

"Later," Sydney said.

Coen sighed.

Sydney scooted closer to him and rested her hand on his thigh. Her friends started talking about Thatcher's recent art show but Sydney wasn't listening. She stared at Coen's face, unable to believe that she ended up with a guy she always wanted. He was everything to her. She felt comfortable challenging him, arguing with him, because she knew they'd always work out there differences. Coen was head strong and aggressive, but he was also passionate and devoted to her. Now she wished they were home and in the bedroom.

Sydney finished her salad then grabbed her bag. "I'll see you later," she said to Coen. She kissed him on the cheek when she stood up.

"What the fuck was that?"

"What?" she asked.

He stood up and grabbed her face, kissing her hard. "I'm your husband so kiss me like I am."

She smiled. "You were talking."

"You can interrupt me for a kiss." He leaned closer to her. "You can interrupt me for anything."

"Okay."

"Will you be home on time tonight?"

"I'll try."

He glared at her. "You have to feed me."

"You can feed yourself."

"No, that's why I got married."

"You survived before. You'll survive after."

He sighed.

"There's leftover lasagna in the refrigerator."

"I guess I'll take it."

She kissed him once more before she left the cafeteria, feeling his eyes drill into her back and ass. Coen blatantly stared at her in class and was affectionate whenever he felt like it. Their rings of eternal love and their tattoos weren't enough.

Sydney went to her next classes and wrote down every word of the lectures in her notes. She sat in the front row like she always did, being the obvious overachiever. She knew it annoyed people. If it annoyed her husband, it obviously irritated everyone around her.

When she was done, she had a break before she left for work. Coen was in class so she took a seat at the table. She took out her notes and started to go through them, her eyes glued to the page.

"Hey."

She looked up and saw Aaron. "Hi..."

"Can I sit down?"

"Uh..."

Aaron took a seat. "I wanted to say congratulations on your wedding day."

"Oh," Sydney said. She wasn't expecting that. "Thank you."

"Coen's a lucky guy."

She nodded. "I love him very much."

"So, how have you been, other than getting married?"

Sydney felt awkward. Just talking to Aaron made her feel like she was cheating on Coen. She'd be annoyed if she saw him spending time with an ex. "Good. Just work and school."

He nodded. "Cool. Are you still living at the shack?"

"Coen and I both live there." She didn't need to add that but she felt like she should.

"I think I gave you the wrong impression," Aaron said. "I just wanted to talk to you as a friend. I really am happy for you."

She breathed a sigh of relief. "I'm sorry I'm being so hostile."

"I understand. I was pretty forward the last time we spoke."

"So, are you seeing anyone?"

He shook his head. "Not seriously. I've been talking to a few girls, playing the field, I guess."

She nodded. "Well, there are a lot of pretty girls here."

He stared into her face. "You're right about that."

Sydney averted her gaze. "I should probably get to work."

"Are you still pursuing a PhD?" It was like he hadn't heard a word she said.

"Yes, if everyone will have me," she said with a laugh. She packed her belongings and intended to sit in the car until her shift started. She didn't want to risk being seen with Aaron by anyone she knew. It would get back to her husband, who would be livid.

"I'm sure you're the most qualified candidate," he said with a smile. "I wouldn't worry about it."

Sydney was about to stand up when she saw Coen's friend, Dan, across the room. They worked at the gym together and were good friends. He was even in the wedding. Sydney cursed under her breath.

"What?" Aaron asked.

"I—I have to go."

"I didn't mean to offend you," he said quickly.

"I'm just in a hurry." She turned down the opposite hallway so she could avoid Dan. But it didn't matter anyway. The damage had been done. When she came home that night, her husband would have a few words to say.

She went to work and started working in the lab, not clocking in until her shift actually began.

Gilbert walked in and stared at her, seeing the experiment in action. "You're crazy, Syd."

"I got out of class early," she lied.

"Maybe I should be the assistant and you should be the lead scientist."

Sydney smiled. "I wouldn't mind the pay."

He opened his briefcase and pulled out a few catalogs. "I wanted you to have these. It's information about the universities I mentioned yesterday."

She took them awkwardly. "Thank you."

"Have you seriously considered it? I'm not implying Hawaii U is a bad place, but there's no guarantee you'll be accepted. There is politics to everything."

"If I don't get into Hawaii U, I don't know what I'll do. I can't just expect Coen to stop living his life and follow me everywhere."

"And he can't expect you to give up your dream for him. Marriage is about compromise. Talk to him, Syd."

She nodded. "I will."

"And if he gives you a hard time, I'll straighten him out. I used to whip him with my belt."

Sydney laughed. "I can't imagine Coen being spanked."

"He used to be a little shit. When he was twelve, he took my car out for a drive then parked it in the wrong spot. The dumbass wouldn't have been caught if he just used his brain."

"That's my husband," she said proudly.

He shook his head. "I'm glad he's grown into a fine man."

"The finest I know." She turned away and finished working, dreading going home that night. She could only imagine how pissed Coen would be about Aaron. She didn't do anything wrong and they hardly spoke about Aaron, but she knew her husband. He was very possessive of her. Anything could set him off.

After her shift was over, she drove home. She hadn't turned on her phone because she knew it would be full of messages and missed calls from Coen, demanding to know what happened that afternoon. When she parked outside her house, she sat in the driver's seat for a while before she walked inside.

When she opened the front door, Coen was standing there, his arms by his sides. His shoulders were tense and he had a maniacal gleam in his eyes, like he wanted to tear down the house just to repair it again.

She sighed. "Calm down."

He marched to her then stared her down. "Why is one of my boys telling me you're spending time with your ex?"

"I wasn't," she said calmly.

He stepped back and crossed his arms over his chest. "Then what happened, exactly?"

"I was doing homework and he sat by me and started talking. The conversation lasted two minutes at the most."

"And what was said?" His voice was low but the annoyance was unmistakable.

"He asked about our wedding and how school was going. It was totally innocent."

He stared at the sincerity in her eyes. "Was he bothering you?"

"No."

"Do you want me to threaten him?"

Sydney rolled her eyes. "No."

"Are you sure?"

"Coen, I can take care of myself."

He sighed. "I'm sorry. Dan made it sound like you two were hanging out. I thought it was odd."

"We just ran into each other."

"Okay," he said. "I'm sorry I got all—protective."

"You mean fucking psycho?"

He smiled. "You like it when I'm psycho."

"In bed."

Coen extended his arms and pulled her into a hug. "I love it when my wife comes home."

She wrapped her arms around his waist and held him close. "I do too," she said. "But it hurts my feelings when you don't trust me."

"I do trust you. That wasn't the issue. I just don't want you to have an annoying ex on your ass. I'd take care of it."

She rested her face against his chest and smelled him. "I'm so tired."

"I made dinner."

"Is it burned?" she asked with a smile.

"It's hard to burn macaroni and cheese."

She laughed. "That's not dinner, Coen."

"It's the best I can do."

Sydney pulled away and kissed him gently on the lips. "I'll whip up some real food."

"Yum."

She put down her bag and prepared dinner in the kitchen. She made grilled vegetables with baked fish and set the table.

Coen ate his dinner across from her. He devoured his fish then ate the vegetables.

Sydney eyed him. "It's better than macaroni, huh?"

He smiled. "My wife's cooking is always better."

She smiled and ate her vegetables.

"Baby, is that all you're going to eat?"

She shrugged. "I'm not that hungry."

"You barely ate lunch."

"I wasn't hungry then either."

He put down his fork and looked at her. "You need to take a step back."

She met his gaze. "What does that mean?"

"You're working too much. Take less hours at the aquarium."

"I'm doing research. I can't just do that."

"Then drop a class."

"No," she said. "I won't graduate on time."

"Drop your ecology minor," he said. "You really don't need it."

"Coen, I'm fine."

He glared at her. "You work all day, and when you come home, you work more. You barely get enough sleep and you're so stressed that you barely eat."

"Well, I can't spend all my time with you. I'm an adult with responsibilities."

"That has nothing to do this," he snapped. "I'm concerned for your health."

"I'm fine, really."

"No," he said. "I'm your husband and I know you're pushing it too far. You don't have time for yourself to relax. Quit your job for the semester. I make enough money as a personal trainer. I can support both of us for the time being."

"Coen, you're making this into a bigger deal."

He pushed his plate away. "I'm not going to change my mind about this. Life was meant to be enjoyed, not pissed away. You don't even have time to enjoy the sunrise or dinner in the evenings. And your health is scaring me. How can someone survive off a salad for lunch and grilled vegetables for dinner?"

"If I was hungry, I'd eat more."

Coen sighed. "We aren't arguing about this. I'll talk to my uncle tomorrow."

Her eyes widened in anger. "Coen! I said I was fine. Don't interfere with my work. I want my name on his paper. I need this for graduate school."

He stood up and leaned over the table. "Then drop a class."

"Stop telling me what to do."

"Too bad," he said. "I respect your wishes but you're killing yourself right now. When was the last time you slept in?"

Sydney left the table and tossed her bowl in the sink. It broke when it collided with the tile. She was too angry to care. She marched to their bedroom then slammed the door, taking out her books and studying. Coen stayed in the living room and didn't come after her, which she was thankful for.

When it was past midnight, she put her books away and set her alarm. She and Coen argued and bickered but they didn't have their first fight until now. She wondered if he would sleep on the couch. She hoped he wouldn't. It would be weird not to sleep with him.

The door opened and he walked inside. He stripped off his clothes and got into bed, lying beside her. Neither one of them said anything. Sydney was glad he came to bed even though she didn't say it.

Coen wrapped his arm around her waist and dragged her to his side of the bed. He kissed her neck while he groped her breasts. Then he grabbed her thigh and raised it, moving his cock inside her.

Sydney moaned as she felt him. He rocked into her hard and fast, rocking the bed. Coen held onto her tightly while he thrust, using his hips to reach far inside. Sydney's body convulsed like it always did when he rocked her world. She gripped his thigh as she screamed.

When they were both finished, Coen snuggled beside her, not pulling out. Her back was pressed to his chest, soft to the touch. He kissed her cheek then her neck before he closed his eyes.

"I love you, baby," he whispered.

"I love you too."

3

Sydney was still mad the next morning. Coen had always been protective of her, but he never told her what to do. Coen was just concerned for her, which was fine, but she didn't like it when he bossed her around. She wouldn't put up with it. It reminded her too much of her stepfather.

When she went into the kitchen, she grabbed a banana and an apple to snack on. Normally, she had breakfast with Coen but she wasn't speaking to him right now.

Coen sat at the table, his coffee untouched. He stared out the window and didn't acknowledge her. His eyes seemed to be empty and dark, like his mind and heart were somewhere else.

Sydney assumed he was equally mad at her. She didn't care if he was. She was right and she knew she was.

When she glanced at the clock, she knew Coen was already late for his first class. "You need to hurry," she said as she put her water bottle in her backpack.

He didn't look at her. "I'm not going to school today."

She stopped. "Why?"

Coen rubbed the sleep from his eyes but said nothing.

"Just because we had a fight?" she said. "That's unacceptable. You need to go."

"That isn't why," he said quietly.

She stared at his face, seeing the depression etched onto his features. "What's wrong?"

He sighed. "It's the anniversary of my sister's death."

His words cut through her heart painfully. She had no idea that was today. They hadn't even been together for a year, so she had never experienced it before. The pain rushed into her and made her heart squeeze. Whenever Coen was in pain, it was a million times worse for her. She came to him then sat in his lap. He didn't push her away. "I'm sorry," she whispered. "I didn't know." She ran her fingers through his hair then kissed his cheek.

"It's okay." He placed his arm around her waist and held her on his leg.

Sydney kissed his forehead then placed her face close to his.

"Baby, you should get going. I don't want you to speed."

"I'm not going to class, Coen."

He finally looked at her. "What?"

"Why would I do after you told me that?" she asked. "Class can wait."

Coen's eyes softened. "I appreciate that, but you need to get to school. I'm just going to sit around and be depressed all day. There's nothing you can do for me."

"That's not true. If you're depressed all day, so am I. I won't leave you."

"No, I want you to go. But my family has a dinner every year to remember her. I need you to come to that."

"Of course."

"And to the cemetery."

She ran her fingers through his hair.

"But I don't need you now. So please go."

"Are you sure?" she whispered.

He nodded.

"Okay." She moved from his lap and grabbed her backpack. "I'll see you later."

"Okay."

She wrapped her arms around his shoulders. "I love you."

"I love you too."

She left the house and went to class. She tried to concentrate but she was having difficulty. Coen's pain kept coming back to her. She never had the honor of meeting his sister. Even though Coen was younger at the time, he still remembered her passing clearly. She understood his pain because she had lost her own father, but she wished there was more she could do for him.

When she went to the cafeteria, she was still upset.

Henry noticed it. "What's wrong, Syd?"

She wasn't sure if Coen wanted everyone to know. "Coen and I—we're just going through a hard time."

"You seemed fine yesterday," Henry said.

"Well, it's not really a fight between us. We're just having some problems with family. It's personal."

Henry backed off. "Is that why he isn't here today?"

Sydney nodded.

"I'm here for you guys if you need me."

She smiled. "I know."

Derek placed a bowl of mixed fruit in front of her.

"What's this for?" Sydney asked.

"I didn't see Coen in class," he said. "I got his back."

Sydney smiled. "I forget that you can be incredibly sweet."

Paola stared at Derek affectionately. "I can't. He reminds me all the time."

"But you give me sex," he said.

"You better not be expecting it from Sydney," Paola said.

Derek grimaced. "That's so gross. She's like my sister."

Sydney laughed. "Coen would be happy about that."

"So everything is okay between you two?" Derek asked/

"Well, we did get in a fight last night," Sydney said. "The first one of our marriage."

"What happened?" Paola asked.

"Coen said I work too much. When I'm not at school or working, I'm studying when I get home. He says

I'm overworked and I need to take a step back from my coursework or research. When I said no, he got upset and the fight just broke out. He's exaggerating."

No one said anything. Her friends ate their food quietly.

"He's wrong, isn't he?"

Henry shrugged.

"Please don't tell me you agree with him," Sydney said.

"You are a workaholic," Henry said. "A bad one."

Sydney sighed. "No, I'm not."

Henry looked away. "It's not my marriage."

"I'm fine," she said. "I have to finish in four years for my scholarship and I have to continue this research if I want a publication. It's a big deal. I can't just take time off."

Ren averted her gaze, and so did Derek and Paola.

"You guys are wrong," Sydney said.

Henry pushed his empty plate away. "I'm sure Coen is just concerned like any husband should be."

"There's a difference between being concerned and being controlling," Sydney said.

Henry fell silent.

"And Dan saw me talk to Aaron yesterday," Sydney said. "So that made it worse."

"What did that fucker want?" Henry snapped. "Did he bother you?"

Sydney rolled her eyes. "Not you too."

"I'll talk to him," Derek said.

"Seriously, you guys are annoying," Sydney said. "I can take care of myself."

Henry looked at me. "If a guy bothers any of the girls, all the guys get involved. That's how this group works."

Derek nodded. "If someone bothered Ren, I'd put them in the hospital."

Ren laughed. "It's like you guys are in a gang."

Paola looked at Derek. "If a girl was hitting on Coen, I wouldn't just jump her."

"Not the same thing," Henry said.

"It sounds like the same thing," Sydney said.

"A girl can't bother a guy. It only works the other way around," Henry said.

"I remember Audrey slapping Coen, stalking him, and making his life a living hell," Sydney snapped. "Yes, a girl can bother a guy."

"Well, that's an unusual situation," Derek said.

Sydney crossed her arms over her chest and sighed. "I just want this day to be over."

Henry patted her on the arm. "Every darkness has to end sometime."

She nodded. "I wish that time was now."

When the lunch period was over, she finished her classes then went by the aquarium. She needed to take out the samples from the incubator and return them to the cabinet. If not, the bacteria would exceed the growth period. She washed her hands then went back to the shack.

Her heart hurt when she walked through the door. Knowing Coen was in pain was excruciating to her. Their earlier argument had been dropped in light of the event. Sydney wasn't one to hold grudges, especially against her husband. She would drop it if he did.

He was sitting on the patio when she walked inside.

She stared at him for a moment before she joined him. "Hey."

"Hey," he said quietly.

Sydney sat in his lap and ran her fingers through his hair. There was nothing she could say to make this better. When her father died, she hated being consoled. The words were just empty, meaningless. Instead, she remained silent.

Coen leaned back and looked at her. "How was school?"

"Derek bought me lunch because you weren't there. He said he has your back."

A slight smile came into his lips. "Tell him I said thanks."

"And he said he thought of me as his sister...even though we look nothing alike."

"Which is why I like him." His mood was a little better when they discussed their friends.

"What time are we going to your mom's?"

"In an hour," he said with a sigh.

I nodded.

"Well, we should get going."

She got off his lap then we went inside. There was a large bouquet of flowers sitting on the table. The flowers were yellow, red, pink, and white. They were different flowers, an eclectic collection.

"They're beautiful," Sydney said when she looked at them.

Coen nodded.

"Where did you find them?"

"Around the island."

She turned to him, surprise on her face. "Did you pick them?"

"Yeah. My sister used to love flowers."

Sydney felt her eyes sag. That was so sweet. Coen was sensitive but she didn't realize just how sweet he could be. "They are lovely, Coen."

"I think she would have liked them." He grabbed them from the table then walked out of the house. Sydney trailed behind him, staying quiet.

They drove to the cemetery in his truck. She sat in the seat next to him, the flowers in the passenger seat. Her hand rested on his thigh. The music was off even though they usually had the radio on. They were both quiet. Sydney wanted to make his pain go away, but there were no words to make that possible.

When they arrived at the cemetery, Coen killed the engine and sat still. He didn't reach for the door, and Sydney didn't move. She would wait until he was ready. He finally opened the door and helped her down. He grabbed the flowers and held them close to his chest.

Sydney held his hand as they walked along the line of graves. When they reached hers, they stopped. The headstone was beautiful. A picture of her was carved into the granite. She was beautiful and lively. Her eyes reminded Sydney of Coen's. Just looking at the sight made her eyes water. It was hard to miss someone you never knew, but seeing their genetic similarities made her heart ache. She was a sister she would never know.

Coen put the flowers down then stood still. He stared at the headstone for a long time, saying nothing. Sydney held his hand and rubbed his knuckles with her thumb. The tears fell down her face but she stayed as quiet as possible. The slight breeze moved through her hair. The only sound was the slight rustle of the leaves. She heard Coen sniff but she didn't look at him. She waited.

Coen wiped his eyes then sniffed again. He swallowed his emotion and regained his composure. Sydney didn't need to see him cry to understand how much he loved and missed his sister. The pain and despair was etched onto his face.

The grave was already covered in flowers. Sydney assumed they were left by other family members and friends. She was never forgotten. Sydney knew she was loved.

Coen placed his arm around her waist and held her close. "Thank you."

She leaned her head on his shoulder.

"This has been a lot easier with you," he whispered. "I know you feel helpless, at a loss of words, but just having you beside me makes a difference."

She wiped her tears away.

"My sister would have loved you."

"And I love her," she whispered.

He took a deep breath then pulled her away from the grave. They got back into the car and drove to Coen's parents' house. They were still quiet. Coen hid his emotion well, but his blue eyes were still dark and lifeless.

Sydney was surprised by the warmth that greeted them when they walked inside.

"Hello, honey," Vivian said as she hugged Sydney.

"Hello," Sydney said quietly.

"Ah-hem," Coen said. "Remember me? Your oldest son?"

His mother rolled her eyes. "Yes, I remember you." She hugged him and held him tightly.

"I heard you had a dinner party the other night," he said.

"It was last minute."

"Just admit that you like Sydney more than you like me."

She pulled away and smiled at him. "I love her just as much."

"Well, that's a little better."

Her eyes softened when she stared at her son, a glimmer of emotion passing.

"I love you, Mom."

"I love you too," she said as she hugged him again.

Sydney watched with a smile on her face and moisture in her eyes. Coen was so close to his family. She was grateful to be a part of it.

Jordan came down the hall and hugged Coen.

Sydney had never seen them embrace each other or even be civil to one another. This was obviously a special occasion.

Jordan pulled away then hugged Sydney.

Sydney returned the affection warmly.

When they came into the kitchen, the food was already laid out. Coen's grandparents were there and they chattered with Sydney for a while, delighted to see her. Gilbert was quiet. He greeted Sydney but didn't say much. Nathan seemed to be taking the day the hardest. He couldn't smile and he couldn't speak. He kept to himself.

When they sat together, they all held hands. Sydney watched everyone bow their heads and close their eyes. She did the same out of respect. After Vivian said the prayer for his sister, they dropped their hands.

Dinner was quiet, not as talkative as it normally was. The tension and despair was in the air. When Sydney looked at the counter, she saw all the pictures of Coen's sister. There was an image of her in her soccer uniform, dance practice, her high school prom. It was a sad sight.

Coen didn't say anything. He ate his dinner, his eyes downcast to his plate. Sydney watched him discreetly, making sure he was doing okay. Even though he seemed strong, she knew there was a hurricane of pain deep inside him.

After dinner, they gathered in the living room and played board games like they usually did. Everyone wasn't as enthusiastic about it. Coen kept looking out the window, forgetting when his turn arrived. Nathan didn't participate at all, choosing to sit on the couch and watch TV. Sydney felt their pain leak out from every pore. Coen's family enjoyed life and appreciated its gift, but they also felt the bitter despair of reality. Sydney wished she could do something to make everything better, to take the pain onto herself. This was the one time she couldn't do that.

When they left the house, Coen held his mom for a long time. After a second, Vivian started to cry. She held onto Coen while she sobbed. Sydney stepped away and gave them their privacy. Coen was so much bigger than his mother, a head taller and almost a hundred pounds heavier. He held onto her while she gave into her despair.

"It's okay, Mom," he said.

"I just miss her."

"I miss her too."

"She would be so proud of you," she whispered.

"I know."

Vivian pulled away. "Let me know if you need anything, baby."

"I got Sydney. She'll take care of me, Mom."

"I'm so happy you found her." She hugged Sydney and held her tightly. "Thank you for loving my son. We're so grateful to have you."

Sydney felt her heart tug. Coen's family always made her feel loved. Everything that had been missing her whole life was fulfilled with Coen and his family. She had everything she would ever need. "Thank you being the mom I never had."

"I love you, honey."

"I love you too," Sydney said.

Vivian pulled away. "Please drive safely."

Coen nodded and pulled Sydney out the door.

They left the house and returned to the shack. When they walked inside, they went into the bedroom. Sydney had work to do but she abandoned it, knowing Coen needed her. They took off their clothes and got into bed. It wasn't that late, but neither one of them wanted to do anything.

Coen lay on his back and faced the ceiling. Sydney curled up next to him and trailed her fingers down his chest. She knew this would be one of the rare nights when they wouldn't make love. There was too much despair and pain to feel any pleasure. Sydney lied still and listened to him breathe.

"Thank you being so amazing," he whispered.

She didn't know what to say. "I love you."

"And I know you do." He ran his fingers through her hair.

"I'll always be here for you."

"And I'm grateful."

"Are you going to school tomorrow?" she asked.

"Yeah. Life goes on."

She rubbed his shoulders and his arms. "When my father died, I blamed myself until someone made me realize it was the last thing my father would want, for his daughter to suffer for the rest of her life. I know Theresa would feel the same way."

He looked at her. "How did you know?"

"I can tell when you feel guilty and responsible, Coen."

Coen sighed. "If I wasn't a wimp, I could have saved her."

"It was out of your hands," she said. "There was nothing you could have done. There is only one person to blame."

He nodded.

"Whatever happened to him?"

"The fucker is still in jail."

"I'm glad."

He sighed then turned on his side, pulling her to his chest. "I'm glad I never have to suffer alone again. It's such a relief."

"I'll always be beside you."

"I know," he whispered. "It makes everything so much easier. I hate remembering what my life was like before you came into it, like a shooting star that set my world on fire. I never thought my wedding day would be the greatest day of my life. When you walked down the aisle, I wasn't even sure if the moment was real. I never felt so much pain and so much happiness at one time."

Her eyes softened. "We're mates for life. And that's what they do for each other. Always put each other first."

"I'm just grateful that my wife is perfect. I definitely upgraded."

She smiled. "You're so sweet."

"Because I'm your husband," he said. "And I'll always be sweet to you."

"Except when you're an asshole," she teased.

"Well, I do have my moments."

She chuckled. "They are pretty common."

"Just remember that every time I'm an asshole, it's for a good reason."

"Say whatever you want to make yourself feel better."

He pulled her closer to his chest. "I love you with my whole heart, seahorse."

"I love you too."

Coen moved on top of her then pulled her hips toward him.

"We don't have to do this," she said automatically.

He pressed his face close to hers. "Life is too short not to enjoy it. And I'm married to the most amazing girl in the world, my other half. I'm not taking it for granted. I will make love to you every night. It was one of my vows."

She grabbed his face and kissed him. "If you insist."

He smiled at her. "I know you get grouchy without it."

"You're a million times worse."

"It looks like we are dependent on one another."

"It seems that way."

4

The anger Sydney had for Coen had disappeared. As far as she was concerned, it was just a fight and needed to stay in the past. After the day he had, she decided to drop it. Hopefully, he wouldn't bring it up again. Sydney was determined to finish her research and graduate on time. There were days when she hardly got any sleep and barely ate, but it was a necessity. And she loved what she did. That made it a lot more bearable.

When she and Coen walked to the cafeteria together, Sydney glanced at him. He seemed better today. He hadn't mentioned his sister or his family. Everything seemed to be normal again. Sydney was still observant of his actions. She could read him better than anyone. "Everyone says they are here for you if you need them."

He turned to her. "You told them?" The anger was evident in his eyes. "We don't have to tell our friends every little thing."

"I didn't," she said quickly. "I just told them we were having some family problems. I had to explain why you weren't at school."

Coen breathed a sigh of relief.

"I'll always keep your secrets, Coen."

"I know." He squeezed her hand. "It's too hard for me to talk about it. I just want to keep it to myself."

"I understand that better than anyone."

He nodded. "I know you do."

When they came into the cafeteria, their friends were already sitting there. Sydney still wasn't used to not having Nancy around every day. But she was happy for her friend. Because of Thatcher, she was becoming more and more popular. It seemed like they traveled as much as they stayed home. Sydney missed her best friend.

Henry studied Coen's face when they sat down. "I hope everything is okay."

Coen nodded. "Everything is fine."

Derek looked at Coen. "I fed your wife yesterday."

Coen smiled. "Thanks."

He winked.

"Even though I'm perfectly capable of feeding myself," Sydney argued.

"If I didn't bring you lunch every day, you would nibble on a piece of celery," Coen snapped.

Sydney glared at him.

"I'll get us something," Coen said as he walked off.

Henry caught the tension. "He's still angry about that fight?"

Sydney wasn't sure. "I don't know. I think he was half serious, half teasing me."

Ren finished her sandwich. "You hardly eat. I don't get how you do it."

Henry stared at her affectionately. "She isn't a garbage disposal like you."

She rolled her eyes. "I like food. What's the big deal?"

"It's not a big deal," Henry said. "It's really cute."

Ren smiled. "That's better."

"Coen is just looking out for you," Derek said. "Don't be mad about it."

Paola wrapped her arm through his. "If Derek wasn't so amazing in bed, I'd be livid with him all the time. He forced me to move in with him because he thought my apartment wasn't safe. As soon as we got together, he was psychotic and controlling."

Derek narrowed his eyes. "I'm just looking after you, baby."

"Well, living in a bad neighborhood and my diet are two different things," Sydney said.

"You are so argumentative," Henry said. "Just tell him to back off."

"I did," she said. "But we'll see how long that lasts. My husband is the most stubborn man I know. If he doesn't get his way, there is no way."

"He sounds just like you," Henry teased.

Sydney smiled. "I guess that's why we get along so well."

"I can't wait to get married," Ren blurted.

Henry stiffened but said nothing.

"Talk about dropping a hint," Derek said with a laugh.

"No," Ren said quickly, looking at Henry. "That isn't what I meant."

Sydney felt bad for Henry. She decided to steer the attention away from him. "Marriage isn't always a honeymoon. Coen drives me crazy. If we didn't have amazing sex, all the messes he makes, all the times he doesn't put his shit away, and all the times he forgets to turn off the stove would become a divider in our relationship."

"But there's no denying how happy you two are," Ren said.

"Well, of course…" Sydney smiled when she thought about the past few months. She hadn't ever been happier. She wished they had gotten married the day they met. Even then, it still wouldn't have been soon enough.

Coen returned to the table, placing a grilled cheese sandwich, fries, a cup of fruit, and an ice tea in front of her. He stared to eat his sandwich like everything was normal.

"Is this Hometown Buffet?" Sydney asked.

"What?"

"There's no nutritional value to any of this."

He glared at her. "It's call fat and carbs. You need them. Grilled vegetables and fruit aren't going to cut it."

Henry shifted his weight, clearly uncomfortable.

Sydney took a deep breath and swallowed her anger. Now she knew Coen was still mad about their fight the other day. Wanting to avoid a confrontation in front of her friends, she opened the cup of fruit and ate it. Coen watched her but said nothing.

"So, Henry and I are writing a piece together for the paper," Ren said. "It's going to be about Nancy."

"Cool," Derek said. "That's awesome."

"That's all you're going to eat?" Coen snapped.

Sydney flinched at the hostility in his voice. Her friends were just as caught off guard.

"I already told you none of this has any nutritional value."

He leaned toward her, close to her ear. "Eat it. Now."

"Fuck you, Coen."

His eyes narrowed. "You aren't eating enough calories, plain and simple. You don't eat meat so this is what you get. I'm not getting you another fucking salad."

Ren glanced at Henry, silently asking if they should leave.

The tension filled the air.

Derek cleared his throat. "So, does Nancy know?"

Henry looked at him. "Yeah. We're interviewing her. I think the art students will like it in particular."

"I don't tell you what to eat," Sydney snapped. "How would you feel if I made you be a vegetarian?"

"It would be valid if I had high cholesterol and a recent heart attack." His eyes still burned with anger. "You aren't eating enough, Syd. You are going to get sick. This isn't healthy."

"Let's have this conversation later," Sydney said.

"No, we are having it now," he snapped. "You would just tell them about this fight anyway."

"Coen, you are making everyone uncomfortable."

"Then eat your food."

"You are really pissing me off," she said.

"The feeling is mutual."

She pushed the plate away and stood up. "Forget it."

Coen glared at her as she walked off.

Sydney went to the science building and waited for her next class to start. When she saw Aaron walk down the hallway, she grabbed her stuff and bolted into the bathroom. The last thing she needed was for Coen to hear about another interaction with him.

Sydney stared at her face in the mirror and tried to control her anger. She understood Coen's opinion. She hadn't been eating like she normally did. She was just too tired and stressed to feel any appetite. But telling her what to do, forcing her to eat when she wasn't hungry, and ridiculing her in front of her friends was unacceptable. She wouldn't put up with that. They were equally passionate and headstrong, which made them both enormously stubborn. But Sydney wouldn't give in.

When she went to the aquarium after school, she immediately got to work. Their experiment had been successful the night before. She streaked the bacteria onto isolated plates then returned them to the incubator. When she diluted the salt concentrations, she checked the levels then recorded her data. The dilution method by the sharks was fascinating. The only problem was, Sydney didn't understand how this phenomenon could be applied to humans. If there was some way the salt concentration in humans could be limited by some sort of drug, diluting it, it would help the diet of millions of Americans. But Sydney also thought good dietary practices would solve all of that. Unfortunately, most people didn't feel the same.

As the evening continued on, Sydney inserted the data into the computer. When everything was recorded, she looked at the time. Her shift was almost over. She dreaded going home to her husband, but she was eager to finish a paper that was due soon.

Gilbert opened the binder and looked at the readings. "Something isn't right."

"What do you mean, sir?"

He glared at her.

"I mean, Gilbert," she corrected.

"Were the glasses cleaned properly?"

"Yes," she said.

He thought for a moment. "Was the salt concentration a hundred to one?"

"Each specimen was ten to one." She opened the procedure and showed it to him.

He sighed. "I apologize. I forgot to mention it needed to be changed." He took out his pen and marked her lab notebook. "We need to do it again."

Sydney sighed. She had already been there all night.

"You run along, Syd. I'll take care of it."

"What? No. We're a team."

"And I know you are still a student that has class early in the morning."

Sydney shook her head. "I'm not leaving. We can get this done much faster if we work together."

He eyed her. "If you get tired, you are free to go."

She turned to the glassware and repeated the experiment. With Gilbert's help, they were able to complete it in less than three hours. Normally, it took her five. By the time they were done, it was midnight. Now she knew she was in worse trouble with Coen. Her phone was in her purse and she forgot to call him to let him know she would be late. Now she didn't want to go home even more.

After they locked up the lab, they left the building and walked to their cars.

Coen was standing in front of her car, his arms crossed over his chest.

Sydney sighed when she saw him. This was going to be bad.

"You got nothing else to do than wait for your wife all night?" Gilbert asked.

Coen didn't look at him. His eyes were on Sydney. "Goodnight, Uncle."

Gilbert got into his car then drove away.

Sydney stood in front of Coen, her gaze averted. He didn't speak or move, but he was frightening to look at. His shoulders were tense and his eyes were bright with menace. She knew how mad he was by the look alone.

He grabbed her purse and pulled it from her shoulder.

"What the hell are you doing?"

He took out her phone and went through it. "Well, it's working."

She sighed. "We had to work late. I couldn't just leave."

"And that's fine," he snapped. "But a fucking courtesy call would have been nice."

She looked at the ground.

"Look at me," he snapped.

Sydney met his gaze.

"It's past midnight," he said. "Do you have any idea how worried I was?"

"I said I was sorry."

"All you had to do was send a text message. I would have been fine with that."

She glared at him. "Coen, we got caught up in something. I can't just leave and make a phone call."

"It's my uncle. Yes, you can leave and call your husband, telling him you'll be late. That's completely appropriate."

She shrugged. "I said I was sorry. What more do you want?"

"I want it to never happen again," he snapped. "That's it. You're constantly running around. I can't keep track of where you are. But late at night, I would like to be updated. What if someone grabbed you when you walked to your car? What if you were in an accident? My paranoid mind works in overdrive."

"I can take care of myself."

"I'm getting really fucking sick of hearing that," he snapped. "We're married now, so no, I take care of you. You take care of me. We're a team. If I was out late, I know for a fact you would be just as livid as I am right now. Don't act like you wouldn't."

She crossed her arms over her chest, closing herself off.

"So, is it going to happen again?"

"I can't promise that it won't."

His eyes narrowed.

"But I can promise that I'll always try to remember."

"That's good enough for me." He walked into his truck and slammed the door.

Sydney walked to her Jeep and got inside. Coen waited for her to leave first like he always did.

When they got home, Sydney opened her laptop and started to work at the kitchen table.

Coen stared at her. "Are you fucking kidding me?"

"I have a few things to do before bed."

His hands curled into fists. "Have you eaten dinner?"

"No," she said. "But I'm not hungry."

He glared at her.

"Coen, not now. I'm too tired to argue."

He left the room and returned a moment later. He tossed a pregnancy test on the table.

She eyed it. "Coen, I'm not pregnant."

"Take the test."

"What the hell is wrong with you?"

"It would explain why you aren't eating and why you're so tired all the time."

"Coen, I'm—"

"Just take it."

She controlled the angry words before they left her mouth. She grabbed the test and walked into the bathroom. After taking it, she confirmed what she already knew. She handed it to him when she walked out. "I'm not pregnant."

He stared at it. "Then you're just unhealthy."

She ran her fingers through her hair. "Coen, I'm already stressed out as it is. All you're doing is making it worse."

He stared her down. "I care about you, baby. That's all."

"I know, but you're crossing a line. Back off."

Coen gripped the edge of the table before he walked to their bedroom. "I guess I'll see you next week." He slammed the door.

5

When Sydney woke up the next morning, her head was resting on the kitchen table. She must have fallen asleep last night after she finished her work, too tired to walk to the bedroom. Coen came inside and made himself a cup of coffee.

"You're going to have a kink in your neck," he said simply.

Sydney rubbed the sleep from her eyes.

He set his coffee down then started to rub her shoulders and neck.

Sydney felt the soreness of her muscles. She moaned as she felt him touch her.

Coen dropped his hands then grabbed his backpack. "I guess I'll see you around."

She sighed sadly, knowing Coen was still pissed at her. She got ready for the day then went to school. She had a quiz in her zoology class, which she felt confident about. When she went to her molecular biology class, she dreaded seeing her husband. They wouldn't speak, but his anger would be palpable.

She walked inside then took her seat next to him, not looking at him.

He placed his hand on the back of her neck and rubbed it. "Does it still hurt?"

She was surprised by his gentleness. "It feels a little better."

His hands rubbed her neck and shoulders, making her relax. "Did you finish all your work last night?"

"I think so."

Coen dropped his hand then rested it in his lap.

Sydney didn't know what to say. For the first time, she felt awkward around Coen. She hated fighting with him and just wanted to forget it. She knew he meant well, but that didn't mean he didn't piss her off. And she understood why Coen was angry with her. He had a valid reason.

The professor started lecturing, and Sydney forgot about Coen for a moment. She scribbled her notes and stared at the board. Coen made notes but his were much different than hers. He drew pictures more than words, and the notes he did take were short and to the point. Sydney wrote down everything the professor said. They had very different ways of thinking.

When class was over, they walked to lunch.

Coen placed his hand around her waist and held her close.

Feeling him touch her made the anger dissipate slightly. It was hard to stay upset when she loved him so much. They went into the cafeteria and sat down.

"What do you want for lunch?" he asked her.

"Just a salad."

His eyes narrowed but he held his tongue. "I'll be back."

Her friends watched him leave.

"I can't believe you actually tamed him," Henry said.

"He's still mad," she said. "I didn't get off work until really late and I forgot to tell him."

"So the honeymoon phase is officially over?" Ren asked.

"We're just arguing right now," Sydney said. "He made me take a pregnancy test because I'm tired and have no appetite."

"Are you pregnant?" Paola blurted.

"No," Sydney said quickly. "Coen is just being annoying." She covered her mouth and started coughing, feeling the sting in the back of her throat. She sniffed when her nose started to drip.

"Do you need some water?" Henry asked, handing her his bottle.

She coughed again. "No, thanks. I have my own." She pulled out her water bottle and took a drink." When she put it down, she started to cough again.

"You're coming down with something," Derek said.

"No, I'm not," Sydney said quickly. "I never get sick." She coughed again.

Henry grimaced. "No, you're getting sick."

"Don't tell Coen," she said as she cleared her throat.

"Why?" Derek asked. "Because you'll have to admit he's right?"

Sydney glared at him.

Coen returned to the table and placed the food in front of her. He brought a salad like she requested. He took a bite of his sandwich then leaned back in his chair.

Sydney felt the tingle in the back of her throat, the undeniable necessity to cough. She drank from her water and tried to ignore it. Unable to hold it back, it escaped from her lips. She covered her mouth then acted like nothing happened.

Coen eyed her but didn't comment.

Her friends started talking, and Sydney ate her food quietly. The need returned and she coughed, covering her mouth. It was deep and guttural. She recovered quickly then ignored Coen. Her friends all looked at Coen, wondering what he would do.

Sydney caught again.

"Do you need more water?" Coen asked simply.

"No," Sydney said. She waited for him to berate her but he never did. She was surprised by his silence.

After lunch, she went to her afternoon classes then to work at the aquarium. She kept coughing. It wouldn't stop. She even bought cough drops but that didn't seem to help. As much as she hated to admit, she knew she was sick.

"Hello, Dr. Goldstein," she said when she walked in.

"What are you doing here?" he asked. "I thought you were sick."

"I'm not," she said quickly. Another cough attack happened and she covered her mouth.

Gilbert raised an eyebrow. "Your husband called me and said you were too unwell to work."

She felt her anger rise. "He was mistaken."

He eyed her. "But you are sick. You should get some rest."

"I'm fine."

"Sydney, please go home. I don't want to get sick."

She sighed.

"And you can have Wednesdays off from now on."

"What? Why?" She knew Coen had something to do with this.

"Coen says you are working too hard. You're suffering at home and you aren't getting enough sleep. I said I can lose you one day a week. It's not a big deal."

"Don't listen to him," she snapped.

"Sydney, I know you are passionate about this and I admire your motivation, but you are still a student. I don't want you to kill yourself over this. I don't think less of you."

"Please, just disregard what he said. I want to be here."

He shook his head. "I'm sorry, Sydney. That's my final decision. Now go home."

She sighed, knowing it was pointless to argue. She grabbed her bag and stormed off, livid with Coen. He went behind her back and sabotaged her work. It was unacceptable.

When she came inside the house, Coen was sitting in the living room. By the resigned expression on his face, she knew he was expecting a fight.

"How could you?" she snapped. Her arms were shaking as she stared him down.

"I had to do what's best for you." He stood up and looked at her. "I'm sorry."

"You're sorry?" she asked incredulously. "You of all people know how important this is to me." She coughed loudly, covering her mouth.

He stared at her. "You are the strongest person I know, Sydney. But even the strongest people need to take a step back and admit when they are overwhelmed. You are drowning right now."

"I'm fine!"

"Sydney, you aren't okay. You haven't been okay in weeks. I did what's best for you. You can hate me all you want, but I really don't care."

"You crossed a line, Coen. This research is important to me. Now he'll just replace me with someone else."

"No, he won't," Coen said. "I made sure of that. He agreed that you work too hard."

"I've worked so hard on this and you're just taking it away."

He looked at her incredulously. "It's one day a week," he snapped. "Just one day! You'll be fine."

She gripped her hair. "I can't talk to you."

"You need to lie down," he said. "And get some rest."

"Fuck you, Coen."

He glared at her. "Don't talk to me like that."

"You betrayed my trust."

"No, I didn't. I had to intervene. You're sicker than a dog. You don't sleep and you don't eat. For a genius, you don't seem to understand the human body very well. Without food and rest, your body can't create ATP to supply energy to the body. And without ATP, your immune system suffers."

"I know basic biology," she snapped.

"Then you know I'm right. You're doing too much."

"I can handle it."

"Obviously not."

"This conversation is over." She marched to the kitchen table and pulled out her books and computer.

"You need to lay down," Coen said.

"Coen, just go away. I'm so pissed at you right now."

"I'm not too happy with you either," he snapped.

She put her earplugs in and ignored him.

Coen went into the living room and started to watch TV.

When she went through her homework, she logged onto her Ecology course to see her most recent grade. When she saw that she was no longer enrolled in the course, she assumed it was a glitch. She logged on again but it did the same thing. Panicked, she emailed her instructor and asked what the problem was. When she read the response, Sydney almost fainted.

"YOU DROPPED ME FROM MY ECOLOGY COURSE!"

Coen turned off the TV. "I had to."

"I CAN'T BELIEVE YOU!"

He stood up and stared her down. "You don't need the ecology minor. You already have twenty units this semester. That's almost twice the amount of a full load."

She felt her arms shake. "That—was—I can't believe you fucked me over like that."

"I understand why you're mad—"

"I'm leaving." She grabbed her things. "I can't even look at you right now."

Coen grabbed her bags and threw them on the couch. "You aren't leaving."

"Get away from me!"

"I'll go," he said quickly. "Stay here."

She glared at him. "Then get out already."

Coen looked at her. "Baby, I hate this as much as you do. But I had to do the right thing."

"This is completely unacceptable," she said. "I might be able to understand the different work schedule—someday—but I'll never forgive you for this. You betrayed my trust. That was just wrong. That's the same thing as going into my bank account and stealing my money, thinking you have the right to take it."

He shook his head. "Not the same thing at all."

"Get out, Coen! I'm this close to slapping you."

Coen stared at her for a moment. "I'm leaving." He turned around and headed to the door.

"And don't come home tonight!"

He slammed the door shut.

Sydney screamed and gripped her scalp. She was so pissed at him. After she calmed down, she contacted the school and reenrolled in the course. Lucky, she was able to fix it since it hadn't been twenty four hours yet.

When she did her homework, she kept coughing and sneezing. Tissues were dispersed around the room. She started to get a headache but she ignored it. Every time she breathed, her chest hurt. She pushed on and studied her notes.

She put Coen out of her mind as much as possible. He kept creeping back against her wishes, along with the anger she felt. When it was late, she looked at the clock. It was almost midnight and he still wasn't home. She expected him to return even though she told him not to. Even though she was angry, she hated it when he wasn't in the house with her. She couldn't sleep unless he was beside her. Sydney was totally dependent on him.

She picked up her phone and called him.

He answered but didn't speak.

"Coen?"

"What?"

"Are you coming home?"

"I distinctly remember being told not to come back."

She sighed. "I'm sorry."

"For what, exactly?"

"For saying that."

Coen was quiet.

"Please come home."

"You want me there?"

"I can't sleep without you," she whispered.

"You slept fine last night," he snapped.

"Just come home."

"Are you still mad?"

"Mad is an understatement. Now get back here."

"Fine."

She heard him jiggle his keys then start the ignition. "Where are you?"

"The beach."

"Were you sleeping in your truck?"

"Why do you care?"

She heard him drive. The faint sound of the radio was on in the background. She stayed on the phone with him while he drove. They fell silent.

When he killed the engine, Sydney walked to the door and opened it. He stayed on the phone until he reached her. Then he hung up.

She stared at him, not knowing what to say.

Coen didn't touch her. He walked past her then headed to the bedroom.

Sydney turned off all the lights and locked the doors before she went to bed. She was still sniffing and coughing.

Coen lied in bed in his boxers and a t-shirt. He normally slept naked.

Sydney opened his drawer and grabbed one of his shirts, pulling it over her head. She lied beside him but didn't touch him. She was livid with him, but she felt better knowing he was next to her. It didn't feel right when he wasn't there.

Sydney set her alarm.

"Are you going to school tomorrow?" Coen asked.

"Yes."

He sighed.

"And I got back into my class," she snapped.

He said nothing.

"Thankfully, I repaired the damage you caused."

"I was just trying to help you."

"Well, don't. I was fine before you came along."

Coen turned on his side, his back facing her.

Sydney coughed again then heaved. She took a deep breath then her chest hurt. She winced in pain.

Coen turned over and sat up, staring at her.

"Stop looking at me," she whispered.

He placed his hand on her chest, feeling her breathe. "Take a deep breath."

"No."

"Sydney, stop being a brat."

She did as he asked. She winced in pain when her lungs expanded.

"Shit."

"What?"

"You have pneumonia."

"No, I don't."

"Yes, you fucking do," he said. "Get dressed."

"Coen, I'm fine."

"If I hear you say that one more time, I'm going to scream."

She flinched at the venom in his voice.

"Now get dressed!"

She climbed out of bed and changed.

Coen drove her to the hospital. Neither one spoke on the drive. Sydney felt her chest hurt with every breath.

She didn't think Coen was right. And if he was right, then she would be in deeper shit.

When they came to the emergency room, Coen guided her to the chair then approached the front desk, taking care of all the paperwork and admission papers. When the nurse took them to the back, Coen kept his arm around her waist and held her tightly. Sydney felt tired and weak, like she couldn't get enough air.

The nurse handed her a gown and told her to change.

Coen sat in the chair and watched her. When she lay in bed, he pulled the covers over her then held her hand, leaning over the bed. His fingers gripped hers tightly. He ran his fingers through her hair and watched over her, his eyes never leaving her face.

They took a few x-rays and blood samples. When the results had returned, the doctor came in.

"Mrs. Marshall?" he asked.

"That's me," she said before she coughed.

"According to tests, you have severe pneumonia, which needs to be treated immediately. The nurse will give you some antibiotics and we'll be monitoring you for the rest of the evening. You came in just in time."

Coen looked at him. "Will she be okay?"

"She'll be fine," he said with a smile.

Coen breathed a sigh of relief.

"We'll release you in the morning." He left the room and closed the door.

Sydney stared at the ceiling, feeling the tension increase. Now she knew she had been wrong. "Go ahead and say it."

"Say what?"

"You were right," she whispered.

"Sydney, I don't give a shit about being right."

She looked at him. "You don't?"

He kissed her head. "I'm just glad you're okay."

Her eyes softened.

"But we need to have a serious talk about this."

She sighed.

"You work way too much. You need to take a step back. I think you should still drop that Ecology course. It's an extra lab you don't need. And you aren't working on Wednesdays. That's final."

"I didn't realize it was so bad," she said quietly.

"It's okay," he said as he squeezed her hand. "I know how stubborn you are. When you are motivated, you become blind to signs you don't want to see. Which is why I'm here. I'm really sorry if I overstepped my boundaries. But I've always had your well-being at heart."

"I know, Coen."

"So, you'll take it easy from now on?"

"I'll be more conscious about it."

"Thank you," he said. "And we're missing something."

"What?"

"You owe me an apology."

"I'm sorry for everything."

"And don't ever kick me out of the house again. By law, half of that house belongs to me."

"I won't," she said. "I was just so upset."

"I know." He kicked off his shoes then lay in the bed beside her.

"You aren't supposed to do that, Coen."

"I don't care," he whispered. "You're my wife. I sleep with you."

"And we definitely can't do what we normally do when we go to sleep."

He smiled. "We could try."

She shook her head. "You're terrible."

"It makes it more exciting that way."

She grabbed his left hand and felt his wedding band. It was smooth and warm, heated by his skin. She loved seeing him wear it. Since they day they were married, he'd never taken it off. And she never wanted him to. She never removed hers, especially since Coen would have a panic attack about it. But that was okay because she didn't want to take it off anyway.

6

When Sydney went home the next morning, she showered then got dressed.

Coen had a look of murder on his face. "You're fucking kidding me, right?"

She stilled. "I'm being treated and it's not contagious. I can still go to school."

He glared at her.

The look made her feel uneasy. Coen got angry about a lot of things, but he never silently threatened her before. She could read the intent on his face, the uncontrollable anger he felt toward her.

He grabbed her by the arm then pulled her shirt off.

"Coen—"

He picked her up and carried her to the bed, placing her under the covers. He pulled off her shorts and tucked her in. "You aren't going to school. Bedrest for a few days."

"Coen, I have class and work to do."

"I'll get your notes," he snapped. "You're staying in bed."

She sighed. "I hate lying in bed."

"This wouldn't have happened if you didn't push it so hard."

Sydney sighed. "Can you get my books and laptop?"

"You aren't studying."

She raised an eyebrow. "Then what the hell am I supposed to do?"

"Rest," he snapped. He grabbed the remote and placed it on the nightstand. Then he removed his clothes and came to bed beside her.

"Coen, you need to go to school."

"I'm taking care of you."

"I'll be fine."

"Why do you always argue with me?" he said, staring her down.

"I don't want you to miss class."

"Who cares?" he said. "School is important, but other things are a lot more important. I'm not leaving my wife while she's unwell. That's much more important to me."

Her eyes softened. "You're such a good husband."

He smiled. "Thank you for finally acknowledging it."

She turned on her side and hugged his waist.

"I'll go by the school and get your notes," he said.

"Thank you."

"Now get some sleep."

She took a deep breath. "I'm so tired."

He ran his fingers through her hair. "I'll make you some breakfast when you wake up."

Sydney hugged him tightly then fell asleep. When she woke up, she heard voices in the living room. It sounded like her friends had arrived. "Coen?"

The door opened and he came inside. "How are you feeling?" he asked.

"I'm okay," she said. "Who's here?"

"Everyone," he said. "They wanted to check on you."

"Well, that was sweet."

"And my mom made you soup."

"Awe."

"My mom never made me soup when I was sick," Coen said. "She loves you more than she ever loved me."

Sydney smiled. "You know that isn't true."

"No, it is true," he said. "But I'm okay with that."

"Did you get my notes?"

"Yep. Everyone got them together."

There was a knock on the door.

"Can we come in?" Nancy asked.

"It's open," Coen said.

They came into the room and approached the bed.

"You have pneumonia?" Derek asked incredulously. "Is it contagious...?"

Sydney smiled. "Give me a hug and we'll find out."

"I'm good," Derek said, taking a step back.

Nancy came to her side. "How are you feeling?"

"Tired," Sydney answered. "And my chest hurts."

"Can I get you anything?" she asked.

"No, thank you," Sydney said.

Thatcher came beside Nancy. "It's a good thing Coen took you to the hospital. He's a good man."

Sydney nodded. "He is."

"It wouldn't hurt to say it once in a while," Coen said.

Sydney rolled her eyes.

Henry sat on the bed beside her and held her hand. "Are you going to take it easy from now on?"

"Now you guys are just ganging up on me," Sydney said.

"Well, Coen was right. You were doing too much," Henry said.

"There's no proof to indicate that's what caused this," Sydney said.

All of her friends glared at her.

"Okay, it probably did cause it," Sydney said.

"You should listen to your husband more often," Nancy said. "He's just looking out for you."

"Did he pay you to say all of this?" Sydney asked.

Derek laughed. "No." He held a folder and dropped it on the bed. "Here are your notes. All of your professors were worried about you, the girl who never misses a class. Their first assumption was you died."

Sydney chuckled, but her laughter turned into a deep cough.

"Gross," Derek whispered.

"Thanks," Sydney said.

"I hope Paola never gets sick like that."

Paola looked at him. "If I do, you better take care of me."

"Baby, you know I'd do anything for you."

Coen walked to the door. "Visiting hours are over. My wife needs to rest."

"No," Sydney said. "I'm so bored. Let them stay awhile."

"They have lives, baby," Coen said.

Nancy smiled at her. "We'll see you when you feel better."

"We can play football on the beach and have dinner," Henry said.

"Who knows how long I'll be sick," Sydney said sadly.

"The longer you rest, the quicker your recovery will be," Coen said.

Sydney rolled her eyes then said goodbye to her friends. When they left, Coen came back into the room carrying a tray. A hot cup of soup was on top.

"I'm not hungry," she said automatically.

"Too bad," he said. He placed it over her lap then sat at the edge of the bed. "Come on."

She sighed then sat up.

Coen watched her eat. When she ate half of it, she put down her spoon. He gave her a murderous look. She picked up the spoon and finished all of it. "Good job," he said.

She lied back down and coughed.

Coen didn't move, his hand resting on hers.

"You don't have to stay with me. I know you have work."

"I called in."

"You didn't have to do that."

"I have a million sick days," he said. "I may as well use one."

"Well, you don't need to stay with me every day."

"We'll see how it goes."

She sighed then cleared her throat.

"Is there a movie you want me to rent or a book you'd like to read?"

"No," she said. "Can you open the window so I can listen to the waves?"

"I can do that," he said with a smile. He opened it then returned to her side.

"I hate being sick," she said sadly.

"You'll be better in no time, swimming with the whales and the dolphins."

She extended her arms to him. "Lay with me."

He stripped down to his boxers then lay beside her.

She moved on top of him then kissed his chest.

Coen pulled her back to the bed. "No."

"Excuse me?"

"You're sick."

"So?"

"I can't have sex with you when you feel this unwell."

"I'll feel better if we do," she said with a smile.

"No."

"Come on," she said. "I want you. We haven't had sex in a few days."

"Who's fault is that?" he snapped.

She rolled her eyes.

He held her to his chest and ran his fingers through her hair. "Just relax."

"I would if I just had an orgasm."

"You're being ornery today."

She smiled.

He rolled on top of her. "No kissing."

"That's fine."

Coen pulled off her bottoms and underwear then removed his boxers. Sydney stared at his hard cock, licking her lips. She loved staring at his naked body. Coen leaned back and watched her face.

"You have such a nice body," she whispered.

"I'm glad you notice," he said. "I work really hard."

"You're perfect," she said, running her hands up his chest.

"I'm nothing compared to you." He leaned over her and inserted himself inside her.

"Yeah..."

Coen moved deep inside her, rocking her gently.

Sydney gripped the headboard as he held her legs back and thrust.

Coen didn't press his face close to hers like he normally did. He kept his distance, not letting her breathe on him.

Sydney grabbed his hips and pulled him into her harder, biting her lip. "Right there."

He moved harder. "Come on, baby."

It hit her like a wrecking ball. She moaned loudly, digging her fingers into his sides. "Yeah..."

Coen met his bliss at the same moment, watching his wife love his body. His moans were loud and guttural. He pulled out a second later and got dressed again. "How was that?" he asked.

Sydney said nothing.

He turned to look at her and realized she had already fallen asleep.

7

Sydney was too ill to go to class the entire week. Every time she tried to leave for school, Coen forced her back to the bed. He always made sure she had all of her notes and necessities so she wouldn't fall behind. But Coen couldn't abandon school forever so he went to class without her.

"How's your wife?" Henry asked at lunch.

"She's still sicker than a dog," Coen said. "I hope our kids don't get her immune system."

"I think her busy life has finally caught up with her," Henry said. "She must be going crazy lying in that bed all day."

"You have no idea," Coen said. "And she still wants to have sex all the time."

"What's bad about that?" Derek asked.

"Have you ever had sex with a sick person?" Coen asked. "It's pretty gross."

"Then why don't you just say no?" Henry asked.

"When your wife wants you to make love to her, you just do it," Coen said. "Trust me."

Renee looked at Henry. "He has a point."

Derek looked at his phone. "Thatcher says we should do out tonight."

"Just the guys?" Coen asked.

"Yep," Derek said.

"I'll ask Syd if she's okay with it," Coen said.

Derek raised an eyebrow. "Since when did you start asking for her permission?"

Coen glared at him. "It's because she's sick. I want to make sure she's comfortable without me being there."

"Oh," Derek said.

"My wife always comes first."

"That's how it should be," Henry said.

Coen pulled out his phone and texted Sydney.

The guys want to go out tonight.

Are you going?

I want to. But if you want me home tonight, I understand.

As long as you sleep with me, I'm okay.

Thanks. I love you, seahorse.

I love you too.

Coen put his phone away. "Sydney is okay with it."

"Should we go to Tully's?" Henry asked.

"Yeah, we'll watch the game," Derek said.

Paola hooked her arm through his, leaning close to him. Renee was just as affectionate with Henry, her hand resting on his thigh. Coen missed Sydney. They bickered often, but he loved feeling her touch him, claim him. It wasn't the same without her. The scent of her hair was absent and the warmth of her smile was gone. Now he sat alone in his molecular biology course. He usually scribbled love notes to her during the lecture, but now she was gone. He hated the loss. He already knew how much he loved his wife, but it was even more paramount when she wasn't around.

After he was done with school, he drove to work. When he arrived in the parking lot, he called Sydney.

"Hello," she said with a cough.

"Hey, baby. How are you?"

"The same," she said sadly.

"I'm sorry."

"I've been sick for a week. It should be done by now," she said with frustration.

"You have pneumonia, not the common cold," he said with a laugh.

"It's still annoying," she said. "I'm glad my teachers are understanding."

"They know how much you hate missing class."

"What are you doing?"

"I'm at work."

"Oh, well have a good time."

"Thanks."

"Where are you guys going tonight?" she asked.

"Tully's."

"Can you bring me something afterwards?"

"Anything you want."

"Some ice cream."

He smiled. "You never eat ice cream."

"I think it will feel good on my throat."

"Sure. What kind?"

"Surprise me."

They sat on the phone in silence for a while.

"I miss you," he said.

"I miss you too."

"It's not the same when you aren't at school."

"It's probably nice," she said with a laugh. "I'm not there to argue with you."

"I love arguing with you," he whispered.

"I do too."

"Well, I'll see you when I get home. Call me if you need anything."

"Okay."

"Bye."

"Bye."

He hung up then walked inside. After he changed, he checked in at the desk and went over his paperwork. Ever since he got married, he stopped taking female clients. There was no doubt that he would never cheat on Sydney, ever look at another woman, but he didn't want to be put in the situation to begin with. It made him uncomfortable touching another women besides his wife.

When he looked at the paperwork, he realized his next client was a girl.

Coen turned to his coworker. "I think you gave me the wrong paperwork, man."

Tyrese took it then looked it over. "No, this is right."

"I don't take chick clients," he snapped.

Tyrese looked at him. "Dude, we're so booked right now. And the rest of the guys can't accommodate the schedules. I'll try to comply with your request as much as possible, but it's not always going to happen. Either be a team player or find another job." He walked into the back office and disappeared.

Coen sighed in annoyance. Now that he was married, he couldn't afford not to work. He'd been saving his money to take Sydney on a real honeymoon and he needed the cash. He sighed then went back into the changing room. He changed into long sweat pants instead of the shorts he usually wore, and his cut off shirt was exchanged for a normal t-shirt. Sydney always wore a shirt and shorts when she went swimming with friends without him, when guys were around, so he had to do the same for her.

He walked into the training room and set up for the session. When his client walked inside, he sighed in annoyance. She was wearing a sports bra and black leggings. Her hair was down, curly at the ends, and her face was pounded with makeup. Coen was immediately irritated. She should be here to workout, not show off.

"I'm Coen," he said simply.

"Casey," she said. She extended her hand to take his.

Hesitantly, Coen shook it.

She had dark brown hair and blue eyes. She had a slim build, with long legs and a lean torso. He couldn't deny that she was attractive, even though she wasn't his type at all.

"Let's get started," he said. "Are you a beginner?"

She shrugged. "I guess."

"And what do you need this training for?" He looked at the clipboard.

"Personal," she said vaguely.

Coen wasn't convinced. "Is someone bothering you, Casey?"

"No," she said quickly, averting her gaze.

Coen caught the lie. "As your trainer, you can confide personal information to me. It will remain confidential. And the more I know about your needs, the better I can help you."

She placed her hands on her hips but remained mute.

Coen thought of Sydney. She was the exact same way when they first met, untrusting, quiet. "Let's begin," he said.

He showed her the basic moves of self-defense, how to block attacks and unleash her own. She seemed to have a good understanding of the practice, but she needed to work on her timing and her confidence.

When he demonstrated moves to her, he never touched her. He wanted to avoid it as much as possible. His relationship with Sydney was solid, and there was no room for any doubt of his commitment to her, but he still wanted to cover his ass.

Casey sweated through the whole training session, and her layers of makeup started to peel away. Coen noticed the slight discoloration around her lips and near her eyes, like they were old bruises. The makeup hid them well, but the abrasions were evident when it disappeared.

When the session was over, Coen looked at her. "If someone is hurting you, you should report it to the police."

"No one is bothering me," she said quickly.

Coen sighed in annoyance. He should just let it go. It wasn't his problem. But his conscious kept pulling him back. It was his duty and obligation to help those who couldn't help themselves. After his sister passed away, he vowed to stop it from ever happening again. "Please talk to me," he said with a sigh.

She flinched. "There's nothing to tell."

"I can see the bruises on your face. I'm not stupid."

Her eyes widened in fear.

"I won't tell anyone," he said quickly. "But please let me help. I've helped many women escape their abusers. I can help you too."

She tucked a strand of hair behind her ear. "I'm fine."

Coen sighed in annoyance. He turned to the cabinet and pulled out a business card then scribbled his number on the back. He handed it to her. "If you need help, please call me. I live five minutes from here."

She stared at him for a moment before she took the card.

Coen wished he could do more, but he couldn't help someone who didn't want to be helped. At least she took the card.

They walked to the front desk where she checked out.

"Thank you for the session," she said as she smiled at him.

Coen rested his left hand on the counter, in plain sight. His wedding band shined under the florescent lights. "Of course."

"Bye." She left the building and walked to her car.

Coen watched her go with a heavy heart. He sincerely hoped that his training would save her life.

He finished the workday with his other clients, and by the time he was done, he was covered in sweat and exhausted. He showered in the locker room then left the building.

He texted Derek. *When are we meeting?*

We're already here.

Be there in 5.

Coen drove to the restaurant and saw his friends sitting at the bar. He took his seat at the end, next to Henry. "What's up?"

"The Seahawks just scored," Henry said.

Coen ordered a beer and watched the game.

"How's Sydney doing?" Thatcher asked.

"She's still really unwell," Coen said sadly. "I might take her back to the doctor to make sure everything is okay."

Thatcher nodded. "I don't mean to overstep my boundary, but is she pregnant?"

"No," Coen said quickly. "I had her take a pregnancy test."

"What does that have to do with anything?" Henry asked.

Thatcher looked at him. "She was tired and had no appetite for a long time. Those are common symptoms of a pregnancy."

Henry nodded. "Well, that must have been a relief for you, Coen."

Coen shrugged. "Having kids scares me, but now that I'm married, it's not so frightening. Sydney would be a great mom. The best."

"If you want your kids to be vegetarians," Derek said with a laugh.

Coen smiled. "Sydney wouldn't do that."

The bartender approached Derek. "This is from the lady in red." He placed the beer in front of him then walked off.

Derek eyed it but didn't touch it. "Now that I have a girlfriend, I get hit on all the time. It's so weird."

Thatcher smiled. "They know you are boyfriend material."

"So you must get hit on like crazy," Derek said.

"It's about the same," Thatcher said as he watched the TV.

"Because you're a dreamy artist," Henry said.

All the guys looked at him, their eyebrows raised.

"I love Ren," Henry said quickly.

They all laughed then looked away.

Coen turned to Henry. "When are you proposing?"

"Soon," he said. "I'm so excited and so nervous at the same time."

"You'll be overjoyed when she says yes," Coen said.

"How did you propose?" Henry asked.

"You were there," Coen said.

"When you did it at school in front of Audrey?"

Coen nodded.

"But that was fake," Henry said.

"Not for me," Coen said. "I had the ring I gave her engraved with her name. I knew I would never want that ring back."

Thatcher nodded. "That's the best proposal I've ever heard."

"Damn," Henry said. "Maybe mine isn't good enough."

"It's perfect," Thatcher said. "It's just right for the two of you."

"How are you going to ask?" Coen said.

Thatcher drank from his beer. "It's a surprise."

Derek sighed. "I'm going to ask her with a surf board. I think that will work."

"Those are all great ideas," Thatcher said.

Coen sipped his beer while he watched the game. It was nice to be out of the house even though he missed Sydney. He wished she wasn't sick so they could go swimming or out to dinner. Her cough attacks made it impossible for her to leave the house. The only good thing was she was getting a lot of work done in bed. She still did research, but she organized data and papers that his uncle would send her.

Someone sat in the empty chair next to him. "Hey."

Coen turned and saw Casey. "Oh hi." He wasn't expecting to see her.

"How are you?"

"Good," he said. "I'm just watching the game with my friends." That was his polite way of getting rid of her. He didn't want her to be abused or beaten, but he didn't want a friendship with her outside the gym. He already had plenty of friends and a wife.

She stared at him for a long time. "Thank you for training me. I was so nervous. I've never done that before."

"I'm just doing my job," he said.

"Have you been doing it long?"

Coen felt Henry stare at him, watching his every move. He was irritated that Henry felt the need to keep an eye on him. "For a few years." He rested his left hand on the table so she would realize he was married.

She nodded. "Were you—ever scared?"

"Scared of what?" he asked.

"Of someone hurting you…"

"No," he said. "Why?"

"Why are you a self-defense instructor?"

Coen would never tell anyone besides Sydney. "It's just a passion. I like helping other people."

"Well, I appreciate all the help."

"You're very welcome," he said. "It was nice seeing you." He dismissed her and waited for her to leave.

She didn't move. She stared past his shoulder and her eyes widened.

"What?" he asked.

"Nothing," she said quickly. She looked at the television.

"I should get back to my friends." He dismissed her again.

"Oh…okay." She slid off the chair then walked away.

Henry was staring at him. "Who was that?"

"A client," Coen snapped.

Henry turned away and looked at the TV.

Coen watched Casey return to a table with her friends. She seemed sad, like his rejection had stung her. He didn't care if she was hurt. He practically waved his marital status in her face. When a man approached their table, large and beefy, Coen watched how Casey cowered. His shoulders tense and her lips lost their smile. Her eyes were hollow and empty. Her friends didn't seem to notice the change in body language. The man gripped her by the arm, yanking her from the chair. Coen felt his heart accelerate.

The man dragged her out of the restaurant. Her friends didn't seem to think anything was odd.

Coen sat there, trying to figure out what to do. It wasn't his problem but he couldn't do nothing. "Shit." He pushed his beer away and walked off. His friends turned and watched him go.

Coen opened the door and walked into the parking lot. When he heard the sound of yelling, he immediately moved toward the noise.

"You said you were staying home tonight," the man said as he pinned her against the door of ha truck.

Casey was shaking. "You said you were staying home tonight too, but here you are."

"I'm a man!" He shook her. "I can do whatever I want."

"So can I!"

He slapped her across the face. "Don't talk to me like that."

Coen ran and pushed him to the ground. His anger burst from his body, giving him adrenaline and strength. "Touch her and I'll kill you."

The man got to his feet then glared at Coen.

"Leave," he said.

"I suggest you leave, boy."

Coen kept his ground. "Touch her again, and I'll make you pay. A man's strength comes from his protection of others, not his abuse. Leave her alone."

"Who the fuck is this guy?" he demanded, looking at her. "You've been cheating?"

"No," she said quickly.

The man pushed Coen. "Get out of here."

Coen grabbed him by the arm then kicked him in the stomach and the groin before the man could react.

He fell to the ground.

"I warned you," Coen said. "Now go and leave her alone."

The man stood up and stared Coen down. "You're lucky I don't have my knife."

"I wish you did so I could stab you," Coen said calmly.

He threw a punch, but Coen blocked it and returned with his own strike.

"I'm a professional fighter. I suggest you walk away."

"Fucking asshole," the man mumbled. The guy stumbled away into the darkness, getting into his car.

When he was gone, Casey was in tears.

Coen turned to her. "Are you okay?"

She shook her head then moved into his arms, hugging him.

Coen stilled at the unexpected affection. He kept his arms up, not touching her.

"Thank you so much."

"Yeah…"

She cried into his chest. "I can't get away from him."

Coen kept his hands up. He hated it when girls hugged him. He felt like he was cheating on Sydney. "Is he your ex-boyfriend?"

"I wish," she said. "I keep trying to end the relationship but he won't let me."

Coen tried to pull away but she gripped him tighter.

Henry walked outside then stared at Coen.

Coen felt his heart accelerate. He pulled away from Casey. "He shouldn't bother you again."

She wiped her tears away. "I hope so."

"You'll be okay. You have my number if you need me."

"Thank you so much."

"I should go."

"Oh…okay."

Coen walked away then moved passed Henry, going back inside.

Henry followed him. "What was that?"

"Nothing," Coen said.

Henry grabbed his shoulder. "It didn't look like nothing." His anger was shining through his eyes.

Coen stepped back. "Don't touch me."

Henry glared at him. "Answer me."

"It's none of your business what it was."

"I'll see if Sydney feels the same way."

Coen pushed him. "You really think I'd cheat on my wife? I know you've always thought you were better for her than me, but you aren't. Drop it."

"Then explain yourself."

Coen glared at him. "I don't owe you an explanation. It's a private matter."

Henry didn't look convinced.

"I'm pissed that you'd assume I'd betray Sydney."

Henry sighed. "She's my best friend. I'm sorry. It's in my nature to look out for her."

"Have a little faith." Coen walked back to the bar, feeling the anger wash through him. He was glad he spared Casey but he wished Henry hadn't seen it. It didn't look good. Sydney would completely understand the situation.

He wasn't worried that she would get the wrong impression. Their relationship was built on trust. Nothing could break that.

8

When Coen came home, Sydney was already asleep. He put the ice cream in the freezer, did the laundry, and tidied up the house before he went to bed. A bottle of Nyquil was on the nightstand, and Sydney was snoring like a baby.

Coen got into bed then kissed her forehead. He hated seeing her so decimated by the illness. He stared at her for a long time before he fell asleep. His phone rang, waking him up. He grabbed it from the dresser and looked at the number. He didn't recognize it.

"Hello?" he whispered.

It was a woman, sounding frightened. "Coen?"

"Casey?"

"Help me," she pleaded.

His heart raced. He glanced at Sydney, seeing that she was still sound asleep. He left the bedroom then moved into the living room. "Are you okay?"

"He won't leave."

"Your ex?"

"Yes," she whispered. "He keeps trying to break down my door."

"Call the police," he said immediately.

"No, he'll hurt me more if I do."

Coen felt his anger bubble to the surface. "What's your address?"

She told him and he wrote it down.

"I'm on my way," he said.

"Hurry."

Coen hung up then left the house. When he looked at the time, he realized it was two in the morning. Hopefully, Sydney wouldn't realize he was gone. He drove to the address as fast as he could, speeding the entire way. Luckily, there were no cops on the road. He drove up the driveway then jumped out of the car. When he tried the front door, it was locked. Sounds of yelling could be heard inside.

Coen took out his pocket knife then picked the lock. After a few tries, he was successful. He burst into the door then ran down the hallway. The man was trying to break down the door with a bat. Coen realized how serious this was.

He shoved the man to the ground, kicked the bat away, and punched him ten times in a row. The blood poured out of his nose and face. Coen was so angry he could barely control himself. It was his sister all over again. When he finally stepped back, blood was dripping from his knuckles.

The guy slowly got to his feet, breathing heavily. "Why the fuck are you here?"

"He's my boyfriend!" Casey shouted.

"Whoa…wait," Coen said.

"It's you?" the man said.

"She's moved on," Coen said. "Leave her alone or I'll kill you. I swear." He picked up the bat and spun it in his wrist.

The man eyed it warily.

"I suggest you leave and don't come back," Coen threatened.

He moved around Coen then bolted out of the front door.

When Coen looked at the bedroom door, it was caved in from the bat. "Are you okay?"

She unlocked it and opened it. "Thank you so much." She jumped into his arms.

Coen felt awkward again. He stepped back. "Please don't hug me."

She looked like she had been slapped. "I'm sorry…"

"I'm married."

"Oh."

"I'm happily married," he added.

She said nothing.

"If that didn't scare him off for good, I don't know what will."

She fidgeted in place. "Why are you helping me?"

Coen stared at her. "Because I want to."

"Jeremy isn't someone you want to mess with him."

"He is if he keeps bothering you," Coen said. "Let me know if he comes back."

"I hope he doesn't," Casey said. "I'm so sick of this. I need to get out."

Coen stared at her dark brown hair and blue eyes. In the darkness, she looked like Theresa. Maybe it was just his imagination, but that's what he saw. It made his heart hurt. "I'll keep you safe," he blurted.

She stared at him.

"Do you have somewhere else to say?"

"No," she said quietly.

Coen crossed his arms over his chest. "You have my number if you need me. But if this doesn't stop, you should call the police."

"Please don't tell anyone," she blurted.

"I won't call the cops."

"I mean anyone," she said. "I don't want anyone to know. Promise me."

"Why are you trying to hide it?"

"Because it's embarrassing," she said. "I have an abusive boyfriend. I don't want anyone to know that. That's why I came to you, hoping I could take care of it myself."

"I won't tell anyone," he said.

"Promise me."

"I promise not to tell anyone but my wife."

Her eyes widened. "I said anyone."

"I tell her everything."

"No," she snapped.

"She's been through something very similar," Coen said. "She would never judge you."

"Coen, I mean it. Can I trust you or not?"

He sighed.

"According to that paperwork at the gym, everything has to be confidential. I wouldn't have trusted you without that reassurance."

"Okay, okay."

She seemed relieved. "And I didn't know you were married. I'm sorry if I gave you the wrong impression."

"I just didn't want to give *you* the wrong impression."

"She's a very lucky lady."

"I'm the lucky one," he said automatically.

She crossed her arms over her chest. "Now what do I do?"

"Move on," he said. "If Jeremy comes back, let me know."

"Now that he thinks you're my boyfriend, he probably won't show up again."

"I hope so," Coen said.

"Do you do this a lot?" she asked.

"What?"

"Help strangers."

He shrugged. "I guess. It's how I met my wife."

"Why are you doing this?"

He was quiet for a moment. "I lost someone very close to me. I vowed not to let it happen to anyone else." He stared at her. "And you remind me of her. I feel like I have to protect you."

"Who was it?" she asked quietly.

"My—my sister."

"I'm so sorry."

He nodded.

They stood there in silence for a long time.

"I should go," Coen said. "Before my wife notices I'm gone."

"Yeah."

"Will you be okay?"

She looked around the house. "I'll manage."

"Call me if you need anything," Coen said. "*Anything*."

"Thank you so much."

"And please reconsider going to the police."

She didn't respond.

Coen left the house and returned to the shack. When he walked into the bedroom, Sydney was still asleep. He sighed in relief. If he couldn't tell her the truth about Casey, he didn't want her to notice his absence to question him.

He went into the bathroom and washed the blood from his hands. Seeing it fall into the drain just made him angry all over again. The situation was too close to his heart. Guys like Jeremy didn't deserve to live. Any man that hit a woman was a waste of life. Coen wished he could kill him with his bare hands. Theresa's face kept popping into his mind. She was laying her casket, wearing her favorite dress. Her hair was displayed around her face, making her look peaceful and happy. Coen felt the tears in his eyes when he thought about it. He lost his sister but he wouldn't let another innocent girl die. He would protect Casey if it was the last thing he'd ever do. He just wished he could tell Sydney about it. He didn't know how he would hide it from her.

9

Sydney didn't question him about that night. Coen was relieved that she hadn't noticed his absence. It was a situation he was thankful to avoid. Sydney was still sick in bed, coughing and spitting out mucous. Coen became more worried.

"Baby, I'm taking you back to the hospital. You should be better by now."

She nodded. "I'm scared."

He held her hand. "You're going to be fine. I just think we need something stronger."

"Okay."

When they went to the hospital, the doctor diagnosed her with bronchitis.

"How is that possible?" Coen asked.

"It's rare, but it happens," the doctor said. "I'll write you a different prescription. It should clear up in a few days." He wrote on a pad and handed it to Coen. "And here is the verification that she can't be in school for a while."

"Thank you." Coen still felt uneasy. He wanted to help Sydney, but he felt worthless.

The doctor noticed the look. "Your wife is going to be fine."

Coen nodded. "Thank you."

When they returned to the shack, Coen helped her into bed.

Sydney sighed in annoyance. "I hate this, Coen."

"I know, baby. I'm so sorry."

"I'm so glad you haven't gotten sick."

He rubbed his nose against hers. "I'm indestructible."

"That's good to know," she said with a smile.

"Everyone says they want to come over and visit you today."

"They do?"

Coen nodded.

"Good, because I'm so bored."

He laughed. "You guys can play board games."

"You won't be here?"

"I have to work, baby."

"Oh," she said sadly.

"I'm sorry. With you not working, I can't give any shifts away."

"I understand."

He kissed her forehead. "I'll see you later. Call me if you need anything."

"I know."

Coen left and went to school. He finished his morning classes then met his friends for lunch. Henry eyed him, watching his every move. Coen said nothing, wishing he'd look away. This would all be easier if he hadn't promised to keep Casey's secret. She was really putting a strain on his life.

When he went to work, Casey was waiting for him.

"How are you?" he asked immediately.

"He hasn't bothered me."

"That's good," he said with a sigh. "I'm relieved."

"Do you think he'll bother me again?"

"I hope not."

She nodded.

They completed their training until the session was over. When Coen walked her out, she fidgeted with her hands.

"I'm still scared," she whispered.

"Don't be. You always got me."

"I'm so lucky I found you. I don't have anyone else in the world."

"I'm sure you do."

She shook her head. "I really don't. I can't tell anyone."

He sighed. That was the root of the problem. When they kept their secrets, no one could help them. Sydney was the same way. And it took forever for her to finally confide in him.

"Well, have a good night," she said.

"Bye," Coen said.

He went back to work and finished with the rest of his clients. When the workday was over, he was excited to see his wife. They hadn't been spending much time together. Coen took a few extra shifts to make sure they had enough money for their bills, but that took up more of his time, in addition to his studies.

When he got inside the car, his phone rang.

"Hello?"

"It's Casey." She sounded scared.

"What's wrong?"

"When I got home, my place was trashed."

Coen was quiet for a moment. "Did they take anything?"

"No. Everything was just scattered, like they were looking for something."

"Where are you now?"

"Surf Taco," she whispered. "I can't go back there. I'm too scared. I know Jeremy has something to do with this."

"I'm on my way."

"Okay."

He hung up and drove to the restaurant.

She was sitting by the window, looking frightened and scared.

Coen sat across from her. "Are you okay?

She nodded.

"Has he called?"

"No."

"It might be a coincidence."

"I don't think it is," she said. "I need to grab my things but I can't go back."

"I could go for you. Or we could go together."

84

"I don't have anywhere to stay."

"You don't have family?"

She shook her head.

"Friends?"

"I can't ask to stay with them without explaining why. It wouldn't make any sense."

Coen sighed in annoyance. "Then where will you go?"

"I don't know…I'll sleep in my car."

Coen didn't like the sound of that. "You can stay with me if you let me tell my wife the truth."

"No," she said automatically.

"My wife won't tell anyone."

"I said no," she repeated.

Coen was extremely annoyed. "Well, you can't live out of your car."

"I don't have a choice."

Coen knew he was going to regret this. "You can stay with me and leave in the morning before my wife wakes up. There's food, a shower, and somewhere to sleep. I'll be right down the hall."

"You would do that for me?"

"I would do that for anyone who needed help."

Casey stared at him. "I feel horrible for intruding."

"Do you have a choice?"

"I guess not."

"You need to change the locks on your doors before you go back."

She nodded.

"How about we go by your place together?"

"Okay."

When Coen moved out of his seat, he saw Henry standing in line, glaring at him. "Fuck."

"What?" she said.

"Nothing."

Coen walked toward the door with Casey behind him. He was pushed from behind.

"Sydney said you were working," Henry said, madness in his eyes.

"I just got off," he snapped.

"So you are spending time with a girl other than your wife."

"Fuck you, Henry. I'm not doing anything wrong."

"I beg to differ. Who the hell is she?"

Casey looked frightened. "Coen is just a friend. Nothing is going on between us. I know he's married."

Coen glared at Henry. "There."

"Like that proves anything." Henry walked back into the store.

"Who was that?" Casey asked.

"My wife's best friend."

"Oh. I didn't mean to get you in trouble."

Coen walked to his car without speaking. They drove to her place so she could gather her things. Coen looked around the room and examined the damage. Nothing was taken. The big screen TV was still in place. Her laptop was on the ground. There was even a fifty dollar bill on the floor.

Casey walked out with a few bags. "I have everything."

"Let's go," Coen said.

They drove back to her car at the restaurant.

"I'll text you when you can come over. My wife usually goes to bed before midnight."

"Thank you," she said.

Coen wrote down the address. "I'll see you then."

Coen drove home with a heavy heart, not wanting to see Sydney. Henry kept his mouth shut, but Coen knew he wouldn't do it a second time. He was furiously protective of both Sydney and Nancy. Coen was surprised he didn't throw a punch right in the restaurant.

When he came home, Henry and Sydney were sitting in the living room. Everyone else had already left. The board games were still sitting on the coffee table. Coen walked in then sat on the opposite couch. He looked at Sydney but didn't speak.

Her face was unreadable. Her skin was pale and her lips were lifeless. She didn't seem mad or hurt, just blank.

Henry looked livid. He stared at Coen with a look of murder.

Coen patiently waited for his wife to speak.

"Henry just told me something," she whispered.

Coen looked at her. "And what did he say?"

"Last week, you were talking to some girl at the bar for a long time. When Henry followed you outside, you were hugging her behind a car. Then he said he saw you having dinner with the same girl when you said you would be at work. Coen, what's going on?"

"I think it's pretty clear," Henry snapped.

"Can I have this conversation with my wife?" Coen said, glaring at Henry.

"You lost those privileges," Henry said.

"Let him speak," Sydney said calmly.

Coen stared at Sydney. "I love that you trust me so much."

"I'm sure you have an explanation."

He sighed. "Baby, I know this is going to sound weird, but I can't tell you why I was with her today and last week."

Henry raised an eyebrow. "Wow."

Coen ignored him. "Baby, the only reason why I'm not telling you is because I promised I would keep her secret. But I'm definitely not cheating on you. It's nothing like that."

Sydney was quiet. She ran her fingers through her hair. "Have you seen her besides those two instances?"

Coen looked at his hands. "I went to her house that same night when you were asleep. I came back before you woke up."

"And what were you doing?"

Coen took a deep breath. "I can't say."

Henry clenched his fists.

Sydney nodded. "Okay."

Henry looked at her incredulously. "Are you seriously going to believe him?"

"I trust my husband. He wouldn't lie to me or betray me."

Henry shook his head.

Coen felt his heart melt. "Thank you."

"Will you ever tell me?" she asked.

"If she gives me permission to share her secret."

Sydney nodded.

"And she's sleeping here tonight," Coen said.

Henry's eyes widened. "What?"

Sydney stared at him. "Where is she sleeping?"

"In the living room. She needs somewhere to stay. She'll be out before you wake up."

Sydney sighed. "Is she dangerous?"

"I would never put you in danger, baby."

"So you are helping her?" Sydney asked.

Coen nodded.

"Then that explains everything," Sydney said.

"I'm not convinced," Henry said.

Sydney turned to him. "Henry, I appreciate your loyalty to me. But I know Coen better than anyone. He wouldn't lie to me."

Henry didn't respond to her comment. "I should go."

Coen watched him leave without getting up.

Sydney hugged him for a long time before he left.

Coen watched, feeling the anger course through his body. He didn't like his loyalty and devotion to Sydney being questioned. He lived for her and only for her.

Sydney came back to the couch and coughed. "Is she your client?"

He nodded.

"And she's seeking self-defense?"

He nodded again.

"So someone is hurting her and you are protecting her?"

"I can't say."

Sydney stared at him. "You don't need to."

"It means the world to me that you trust me so much."

"And it means everything to me that you don't lie to me."

He moved to the couch next to her and kissed her forehead. "Never trust someone who lies to you, and never lie to someone who trusts you."

"Good words to live by."

He pressed his face close to hers. "I'm sorry you found out this way. I was trying to hide it from you."

"It's okay," she said. "Just be safe, Coen."

"I'm always safe."

"And I'm proud of you."

He stared at her face for a long moment, seeing the adoration in her eyes. "Why?"

"For protecting someone who can't protect themself."

10

Coen was relieved that Sydney trusted him as much as she did. He had to admit that his actions looking nothing but suspicious. If she was anyone else, it could have gone a lot worse. He was grateful he made such a good choice marrying her. The love, friendship, and trust they shared was unparalleled. He didn't even trust his family as much as he trusted her.

When Casey came over, she texted Coen.

I'm here.

Coen opened the door and let her come inside. "You found it okay?"

She nodded. "Thank you for letting me stay here."

"Of course."

"I hope I didn't get you in trouble."

"No, my wife trusts me."

"I'm glad I didn't do any damage."

"I want you to meet her," Coen said.

Her eyes widened. "She knows I'm here?"

"I didn't tell her anything," he said quickly.

"And she's okay with me being here?"

"Like I said, she trusts me."

She put her bags on the ground then looked around. "This is a nice place."

"Thank you."

Sydney came down the hall wearing her pajamas. "Hello, Casey," she said with a smile.

Casey froze. "Hi…"

"There's an air mattress made for you. And help yourself to anything in the kitchen."

"Thanks," Casey said.

Coen nodded. "Goodnight."

"Goodnight," Casey said.

Coen walked down the hall and went into his bedroom.

Sydney sat down on the couch. "Let's talk for a moment."

Casey sat down, looking tense. "Coen and I never did anything."

Sydney chuckled. "I know. That isn't what I wanted to talk about."

Casey eyed her. "You don't feel threatened by me?"

"Why would I? Coen is the greatest guy I know. He isn't a liar or a cheat. No one threatens me."

"I hope I find a relationship like that someday."

"You will," Sydney said. "Coen didn't tell me what happened to you, but since he's a personal trainer, I can connect the dots. I was abused by my stepfather and Coen made me tell him everything that happened. That's how we fell in love."

Casey nodded.

"So I understand exactly what you're going through. Coen and I will help in any way we can."

"Wow. You guys are so…amazing."

"We've both suffered. We like to help others when they need it."

Casey stared at her.

"Tell me what happened."

She shifted her weight. "I—I don't like to talk about it. I only told Coen because he's my trainer."

Sydney nodded. "I understand. I suggest you find a new place to live and move on. You can call Coen if you ever need anything."

"He's saved me so many times. I've never seen anyone kick so much ass."

Sydney laughed. "He's very good at what he does. He trained me."

"Did you…defeat your tormentor?"

"I know I'll never see him again, so yes, I did."

"I'm so glad I met him."

"Coen is a pretty great guy."

Casey placed her hands in her lap. "Thank you for letting me stay here. I have nowhere else."

"You're always welcome here, Casey."

"Thank you. I'll look for a new place tomorrow."

Sydney patted her hand. "Goodnight."

"Goodnight."

Sydney walked into their bedroom and saw Coen lying in bed. She coughed a few times before she lay down.

Coen pulled her to his chest. "You're amazing, you know that?"

"You're the one who's saving her."

"But most other wives would assume the worst."

"But I trust you, Coen."

He kissed her neck. "That makes me happier than you'll ever know."

"I'll talk to Henry tomorrow, calm him down."

Coen shook his head. "Leave him be. He behaved the same way any other person would. I don't blame him for what he did. Your opinion is the only one that matters."

She cuddled next to him. "She said she'll find a new place tomorrow."

"Good," he said. "We'll get rid of her and I can get a full night of rest again."

Sydney chuckled. "You're the most amazing man I've ever known."

He smiled at her. "I like what I'm hearing."

"You are."

"Go on…"

"And I'm honored that I'm spending the rest of my life with you."

"Even better."

She kissed his cheek then rested her head on his chest. "She reminds me of your sister."

Coen nodded. "I thought the same thing."

"So I understand how important this is to you. It's very close to the heart."

"I'm glad you understand me so well."

Sydney sighed then closed her eyes, falling asleep in his arms.

The next morning, Sydney and Casey looked up apartments for rent. Coen got ready for school then poured himself a cup of coffee.

"Any luck?" he asked.

"There are a few good places," Sydney said.

Coen turned to Casey. "Did you sleep well?"

"Yeah," she said with a sigh. "It's nice being able to sleep without worrying about someone choking you."

Sydney gave her a sympathetic look.

Coen kissed Sydney on the forehead. "I'll see you later, baby."

She smiled. "Hurry home."

"I will." He turned to Casey. "I'll see you later."

"Bye," she said.

After Coen gathered all of Sydney's assignments and completed his classes, he went to the cafeteria for lunch. All of his friends were quiet when he sat down. The tension was in the air. Henry stared at him.

Coen ate his sandwich and ignored them. He didn't care what anyone else thought besides Sydney.

Henry cleared his throat. "I apologize for how I acted yesterday."

Coen looked at him. "There's no need for apology. You did the right thing. I would have done the same thing if I saw you with some other girl, not where you said you would be."

Henry nodded. "I just didn't want you to take it personally."

"I don't," he said. "She's your best friend. I understand why you protect her."

"So, is everything okay between you two?" Derek asked.

"It's more than okay," Coen said. "It was just a misunderstanding."

"So, what's the story with this girl?" Henry asked.

Coen sighed. "I can't say."

"Did she stay with you guys last night?" Henry asked.

"Yes."

Derek raised an eyebrow. "Is she homeless?"

Coen shook his head. "She—has special needs. I promised I wouldn't tell anyone her secret and I keep my word. I didn't even tell Sydney, but she figured it out on her own, for the most part."

"I'm sorry I accused you of cheating," Henry said.

"Let's just forgot about it," Coen said.

"Okay."

After lunch, Coen went home. When he saw Sydney, he gave her a big kiss, not caring that she was sick. Knowing she trusted him as much as she did made him even more in love with her. Even if it was his word against the whole world, she would still be on his side. It was the greatest feeling.

"How was your day?" Sydney asked.

"Shitty without you."

"Did you talk to Henry?"

"He apologized."

"I figured he would," Sydney said.

"Did you find a place?" Coen asked.

"We did," Sydney said with a smile. "Now we need you to move everything."

Coen smiled. "Look how that worked out..."

Casey came into the living room. "Hey, Coen. Did Syd tell you the good news?"

"You found a place," Coen said with a nod. "Let's get moving."

"It's going to take forever with just the two of us," Casey said.

"There will be a lot more," Coen said. "Trust me."

Coen called up all their friends and asked for their assistance. Naturally, they were all there immediately.

"Wow," Casey said. "You have a lot of friends."

Sydney smiled. "They are family."

"This is Casey," Coen said to everyone. "She needs help moving into a new apartment."

Everyone introduced themselves and made her feel welcomed.

After they drove to her house, they started packing and placing everything into the cars and trucks.

Casey came to Coen. "All your friends are really hot."

He laughed. "And they are all taken."

She sighed. "Why is that always the case?"

He shrugged. "You gotta snatch them while you can."

"Where's Sydney?" she asked.

"She's too sick to help. I made her stay home."

"Your wife is beautiful."

He smiled. "I know she is."

"And really nice. I've never met people who were so compassionate toward others."

"Well, she makes me that way," he said. "I'm always trying to be a better man for her."

"You guys are too cute," Casey said.

"We try."

They packed everything then moved the furniture into the new apartment. It was a two bedroom place with just enough space. They helped her put her bedroom furniture together and stacked her kitchen supplies. By the time everyone was done, they were exhausted.

"Thank you so much," Casey said. "That was so nice of you."

"Well, when you deal with one of us, you deal with all of us," Derek said.

Casey smiled. "I really appreciate it. I don't have anyone to help me." Her smile faded and her eyes grew empty.

Coen clapped her on the shoulder. "You always have us as friends."

"Really?" she asked quietly.

"Of course."

"Thank you."

Everyone left except for Coen. He stayed behind so he could have a private chat with Casey.

"Call me if he tracks you down."

"I will," she said.

"And when my wife feels better, she'll beat the shit out of him too."

Casey laughed. "She's too cute to hurt anyone."

Coen shook his head vigorously. "She could kick my ass any day."

"Wow. That's a kinda friend I would want to stick around."

"I know Sydney would love to spend time with you when she's feeling better. She's been on bedrest for a while and she's getting pretty aggravated."

"I can imagine," Casey said.

"And she keeps saying she's gaining weight when she isn't."

"Maybe she's pregnant."

"Everyone keeps saying that," Coen said. "She's not. We checked."

"How long have you guys been married?"

"A few months."

"Oh," she said. "So you guys aren't ready for kids."

"No," he said with a laugh. "We can barely feed ourselves as it is."

Casey smiled at him. "Let me know if there's anything I can ever do for either of you. I'd be happy to help."

"You've already helped me more than you'll ever know." He walked out the door and shut it behind him.

11

"I want to go swimming today then we'll go hiking tomorrow. On Wednesday, let's go surfing with Thatcher. And I want to sail. Let's go sailing!" Sydney kept talking about all the activities she wanted to do that week. Now that she felt better, she was extremely hyper.

"Let's just take it one day at a time," he said.

"Let's make love in the shower."

His eyes widened. "I'm not going to say no to that, but you shouldn't do too much, too quick. You remember what happened last time."

She rolled her eyes. "You're such party-pooper."

"I'm just a concerned husband."

She sat at the kitchen table and drank her coffee.

Coen sat beside her and watched her eat her breakfast. After getting sick, Sydney took her nutritional diet very seriously. She ate more than she used to, which was a relief to Coen. He was one step away from force feeding her.

"How's Casey doing?"

"Well," he said. "She likes her new place."

"Has Jeremy bothered her?"

"No. She changed her number so he hasn't contact her."

"That's good," she said.

"Yeah."

"I know Theresa would be proud of you," she said quietly.

"I'm just glad I could spare someone since I couldn't spare her."

Sydney eyed him. "Don't hold yourself responsible, Coen. It wasn't your fault."

"I'll always feel this way. I try not to but it happens anyway."

Sydney grabbed his hand. "You're such a wonderful man."

He smiled. "I'm glad you think so."

"I'm sure Casey does too."

"I do feel better knowing I helped her."

"And you should," Sydney said.

"I hate to imagine what would have happened if I wasn't around."

She drank from her coffee then set it down. "What if you opened up your own self-defense studio, specifically for women? You could be a trainer and a motivational speaker."

"That costs money," he said with a laugh.

"I'm sure we find some investors."

"You mean Nancy?"

She shrugged. "I'm sure she would help. She has more money than she knows what to do with."

Coen shook his head. "That's a hard business. We would have to build up clients before we made a profit. And I would have to hire instructors."

"You have me," she said.

"But you have your own passions."

"I can do both."

He glared at her. "So you can work 24/7 like you've been this semester? No thanks."

"We would figure something out."

"No," he said.

She dropped the argument and finished her coffee. "I need to leave for school."

"Take it easy," Coen said firmly.

She sat on his lap and rubbed her nose against his. "I dropped the Ecology class. You're right. I don't need the minor."

He smiled. "Thank you."

"And I have Wednesdays off with you."

"No, Wednesdays are the days you take for yourself. I'll cook dinner and do the housework. You just lie on the couch and watch TV."

Her eyes softened. "You're so sweet, Coen."

"Because you're my wife and I love you. I would never help my mom out."

"You're a momma's boy and you know it," she said with a laugh.

"What's wrong with that?" he said with a smile. "I love my mom."

"That's so cute."

"I am pretty cute," he said with a wink.

"I need to do something nice for you for being so good to me."

His eyes brightened. "What did you have in mind, baby?"

"Why don't you pick?" She rubbed his shoulders.

"Ooh...this could take a while."

"Take your time."

He smiled. "This is going to be the best week ever."

She moved from his lap then grabbed her bag. "I'll see you at lunch."

"Bye."

Sydney went to her classes and submitted her late work. Her professors were understanding since she was legitimately sick. She scheduled her make up exams that week, but she didn't feel nervous for them. She'd been doing nothing but studying in bed. Her lab professors waved her points and her lab write ups.

At lunch, Sydney sat down with her friends.

"Happy to be back?" Henry asked.

"You have no idea," she said with a sigh. "It's nice to walk around. And I was gaining weight since I was lying in bed all day."

"Or maybe you're pregnant," Ren said.

Sydney laughed. "I'm not pregnant! Coen made me take a test three times."

Ren looked sad. "Oh."

"How's Casey doing?" Henry asked.

"She's happy in her new place."

"I hope she escaped whatever was chasing her," Henry said.

Sydney looked at him. "I think Coen took care of that."

"How did Coen get involved in that?" Derek asked.

"Well, he's a person trainer," Sydney said. "He meets abused people all the time."

"And he helps them?" Henry asked.

Sydney nodded. "It's his passion in life. He wants to help other people, particularly women."

"Wow," Henry said. "I had no idea."

"He's an amazing man," Sydney said.

"And a badass," Henry said. "That's so cool."

Sydney smiled at him. "Now you know why I love him so much."

Coen came to the table and placed a tray in front of Sydney. It was a grilled cheese sandwich and fries.

She eyed it but didn't complain. "We were just talking about you."

"Were you telling them what you are going to do for me tonight?"

Sydney rolled her eyes.

Derek raised an eyebrow. "What's going on tonight?"

"I'm getting some serious loving for being an amazing husband."

"They didn't need to know that," Sydney said.

"Yes, they did," Coen said. "I don't want them calling us while we're humping away."

Ren laughed. "It sounds like a romantic evening."

Henry looked at Coen. "I have new respect for you, man."

Coen met his gaze. "Because I have sex with my wife?"

Henry smiled. "Sydney told us what you do. You protect women that can't protect themselves. That's awesome."

Coen averted his gaze, his cheeks starting to turn red.

"He's right," Derek said. "You're awesome."

"And I feel horrible for accusing you of cheating on Sydney," Henry said.

Coen didn't anything, at a loss of words.

"He appreciates the words," Sydney said. "He's always been very humble about his good qualities."

"Or silent about them," Derek said with a laugh. "I always thought Coen was an ass before I met him."

"I like to keep it that way," Coen said with a smile. "It's the element of surprise."

Sydney placed her hand on his thigh and stared at him affectionately.

Coen felt the look and loved it. His wife could stare at him like that all she wanted.

After the afternoon classes were finished, Sydney went home and hit the books. Coen was working tonight so she was alone in the house. Now that she realized how hard she was pushing it, she decided to take a step back. Dr. Goldstein understood her need to cut her hours, and her teacher didn't question her decision to drop the course. There was more to life than school and work.

There was a knock on the door. The sound made Sydney flinch. She didn't know who it was. Coen wouldn't knock, and her friends would call before they came over. And solicitors never came to her door because it was hidden from the road by the trees.

She walked to the door then looked through the peephole. Her heart raced when she saw the face on the other side. It was so unexpected that it made her shake.

She opened the door. "Mom, what are you doing here?"

Her mother's bags were at her feet. She looked thin, like she had lost substantial weight. Her clothes were baggy, and her hair was unkept. What light she had in her eyes was gone. She looked like a shadow of the woman she used to be. "Hello, honey," she said quietly.

Sydney immediately scanned the yard, looking for her stepfather and brother.

"I'm alone," she said.

Sydney stared at her. "Mom, what are you doing here?"

"I—I couldn't stay there any longer. It got worse…"

Sydney felt her heart ache.

"I had to get out. And—I have nowhere else to go. You're the only family I have, Sydney."

She didn't know what to say. The shock still gripped her. "I'm so sorry, Mom. Are you okay?"

She nodded. "I will be eventually."

Sydney stood still, frozen in place. Her heart slammed in her chest.

"Can I come in?" she asked.

"Oh…yeah, of course." She gathered the bags and helped her mother inside. After she shut the door, she locked it.

Her mother looked around. "You've decorated it well."

Sydney wasn't expecting the compliment. Her mom usually tore her apart. "Thank you."

"How's your husband?"

"He's good," Sydney said.

"He's a fine young man."

"I know."

Denise sat on the couch and sighed.

"What happened?" Sydney asked.

"Dan has only gotten worse. He lost his job because of his drinking, and when he got it back, they demoted him to a lower position. He's been taking it on me. I just got sick of it and ran. I couldn't be there any longer, not if I wanted to live."

Sydney grabbed her hand. "It'll be okay, Mom."

Her mom started to cry.

Sydney held her in her arms and patted her back. "You're safe here."

"Thank you so much," she said through her tears. "You're so wonderful, Sydney. I don't know you became the amazing woman you are now. But I know it has nothing to do with me."

Sydney couldn't disagree more. It was those horrific experiences that made her become strong. "Can I get you some tea or water?"

"I'm okay," she said as she pulled away.

"Let's get you settled," Sydney said. "I have an air mattress you can have."

"Thank you so much," she said. "I have nowhere else to go."

"You're always welcome here, Mom."

She nodded, tears still falling down her face.

Sydney helped her mom get settled in the house. It was awkward for a few hours. Sydney wasn't sure what to say or how to act. She had never been close with her mom, and for most of her life her mother was someone she didn't like. But now she was here, begging for her help.

They made dinner together and made small talk.

"How's school?" she asked.

"I like it," Sydney said. "I've been doing research at the aquarium."

"That's wonderful," she said. "I'm happy for you."

Sydney was surprised once again.

"How's the marriage?"

"We're very happy," Sydney said.

"Does he go to the same college?"

Sydney nodded.

"What have you been doing lately?"

"Well, I was sick for a long time. I was pretty much handicapped for weeks. Coen had to take care of me."

"I'm sure he didn't mind," she said. "Are you still a vegetarian?"

"Forever and always," Sydney said.

"You'll live to be two hundred," her mother said with a smile.

When dinner was ready, they left it on the stove and moved to the living room. They watched TV in silence. They were waiting for Coen to come home before they sat at the table.

The front door opened, and Sydney knew her husband was home.

"That smells great," he said as he put his bag down by the front door. He came into the living room and kissed Sydney, unaware of her mother sitting across the room. He grabbed her face and deepened the kiss. Sydney knew what that touch meant. She pulled away.

"Hey, how was work?"

"Long," he said.

"We have company."

"Oh." He turned and saw her mother. He froze, staring at her.

Sydney felt the tension pick up. "She's going to be staying with us for a while."

Coen looked angry, livid. "Let's talk outside." He walked out the front door and slammed it behind him.

Sydney looked at her mother. "Uh, I'll be right back." She followed him outside and saw him pacing in the yard. "What's wrong?"

He turned to her, a glare on his face. "What the fuck is she doing here?"

"Dan isn't here," she said immediately.

"Obviously," he snapped. "And that isn't what I asked."

"She left him."

"And came here?"

Sydney stared at him incredulously. "She has nowhere else to go."

"That's not my fucking problem!"

"Why are you acting like this?"

He came to her then stared her down. "And you think Dan isn't going to come looking for her?"

"Well…"

"He will," Coen said. "And I'm not letting him near you ever again. She isn't staying here. That's final."

"Coen, she needs our help."

His eyes shined with flames. "Where was she when you were being beaten with a baseball bat? Where was she when Johnny would molest you? Where was she when Dan would verbally abuse you, calling you a bitch and a brat? I don't give a shit if she needs our help. She did this to herself."

Sydney blinked back her tears.

"You don't owe her anything, Syd."

"She's my mom…"

"I don't care. You have the same blood but you aren't family."

"She's changed."

"People don't change," he snapped. "Dan is going to come here and drag her by the hair, coming near you. I can't let that happen."

"What happened to helping others who couldn't help themselves?"

His eyes grew dark. "How dare you say that to me! This woman let Dan break your ribs. She doesn't deserve to be saved."

"You don't believe that," she said with a sniff.

His voice became quiet. "Baby, I know how selfless you are. You need to help everyone. But this is not one of those times. Having her here is putting you in danger, which I can't allow. She can't stay here, Syd."

She crossed her arms over her chest and looked away.

"I want her out of the house."

"I can't just kick her out."

"I'm not going to risk your life for hers."

"She's your family too."

His eyes narrowed. "She's no family of mine. I generously allowed her to come to our wedding. That's it. She isn't living with us."

"And if I turn her away, where will she go?"

"I don't care," he snapped. "You were abused until you became an adult. You had no money, no family, and no protection. Look where you are now. You had to start with nothing. Now so does she."

"Coen, I know you're trying to do what's best for me, but I can't reject someone that needs help. I just can't."

He gripped his scalp, taking a deep breath. "Fine. You aren't living here then."

"What?" she asked incredulously.

"You can stay with Nancy and Thatcher while I stay here with her. I'll get her back on her feet, and when she leaves you can come back. When Dan comes to drag her away, I'll protect her. But you can't be here when that happens."

"But—no. We are married, Coen. We can't live apart."

"There's no other way. I'm not letting her stay here. You have to decide what you want to do."

"Neither one of those options is good."

"Then pick the lesser of two evils."

"Coen—"

"I'm not going to change my mind."

"What if we find her another place to live?"

"With what money?" he snapped. "We can barely afford our own expenses."

"We'll get her a job and help her get a place."

"I have a strong feeling your mother isn't employable."

"Coen, we'll figure it out."

"Fine. But for the time being, you aren't living here. I'll move your stuff to Thatcher's."

"You can't be serious!"

"I'm not letting you stay here. When they come back, I don't want you near them. I'm your husband and I take care of you."

"I can take care of myself," she said. "You know that."

"But you shouldn't have to do. You've put this life behind you. I'm not going to let it haunt you. That's the plan. I can't be negotiated with."

"This is insane."

"Then tell her to leave."

"I can't do that."

"Then this is the plan."

She sighed. "I'm not telling her that."

"I have no problem setting the record straight," Coen said.

"Don't be rude to her."

"I took a bat to the chest, which could have caved my sternum in. I can be rude to her if I feel like it. It was selfish of her to come here and put you in danger. She doesn't care about you, Sydney. She just wants us to protect her, feed her, and house her."

"That isn't true."

He shook his head. "I admire your ability to see the good in people even when there is none there, but in this instance, it's pure ignorance." He walked back to the house, leaving Sydney on the verge of tears.

She followed him inside and watched him sit on the couch next to her mom.

"Hello," he said. "I'm sorry I didn't say hi earlier."

"Hello," she said. "Thank you for letting me stay here. My daughter has a wonderful husband."

He nodded. "Thank you. Sydney and I are going to get you a job and an apartment. Sydney won't be living here for the time being. It will just be you and I."

Her mother looked confused. "Why?"

"I don't want your husband near my wife," Coen said firmly. "He abused her for years. She'll be staying with friends until you're out of the house."

She looked at Sydney. "Is this true?"

Coen turned to her, waiting for her to agree.

"Yes," she said.

"I—I didn't come her to complicate your lives," she said quietly.

Coen looked at her. "Sydney and I will help you in whatever way we can. But my wife is my number one priority. As long as you're here, her safety is at risk. The sooner you find a job and leave, the less of a burden you'll be."

"Coen!"

"I don't care," he snapped. "She didn't take care of you when you needed it most. If she came here expecting anything less, she's sadly mistaken."

"Don't be rude," Sydney said.

"Too late."

Her mother looked at Coen. "I completely understand."

"Thank you," Coen said.

"He's right, honey," she said to Sydney.

Coen stared at her, surprised by the reaction. "We'll get started tomorrow."

They had dinner together at the table in silence. No one spoke or made small talk. Sydney felt awkward, wishing her mother hadn't caused a rift between her and her husband. She was finally well enough to spend time with him, but now they had more drama in their lives.

When they got ready for bed, Coen made a sleeping bag in the entryway.

"My mom has an air mattress," Sydney said.

"This is for me," he said simply.

"What?"

"I'm sleeping here."

"Why?" she said. "Coen, you need to sleep with me."

"I can't. I'm sorry."

"You don't need to sit in front of the door like watchdog."

"You can't argue with me."

"Then I'll sleep here too."

"No," he snapped. "Go to bed."

"But Coen—"

"He held a knife to your throat while we were sleeping. That still haunts me every night. I'm sleeping here. I can hear everything in the house. That's final."

She sighed, knowing she couldn't argue with him.

He crawled into the sleeping bag, a baseball bat right beside him.

Sydney sat next to him and kissed his forehead. "Come to my room and I'll do that thing you like."

"I'm not in the mood," he said simply. "Go to bed, baby."

"I can't sleep without you."

"It's temporary."

She sighed sadly.

"I'm not doing this to hurt you."

"I know."

He sat up and kissed her on the forehead. "It's my job to keep you safe. And safe is what you'll be."

12

The next day, Coen and Sydney went to Thatcher and Nancy's place after class. Sydney was nervous to tell them the truth of her past, but there was no way to get around it. She wouldn't disrespect her friends by lying to them.

They sat at the kitchen table while Nancy passed around mugs of coffee. Thatcher watched her, his eyes lingering on her hands and wrists. Sydney studied him ,watching the way he gazed at Nancy like she was the most prestigious work of art. She was happy her best friend found a man that loved her so much.

"So, what's this about?" Nancy asked as she sat next to Thatcher.

Thatcher placed his arm over the back of her chair, his fingers touching her neck.

Sydney sighed but couldn't speak.

Coen noticed her unease and took the reins. "We need a favor."

"You know we'd do anything for you," Thatcher said. "Just name it."

"It's complicated," Coen said. "I need Sydney to stay with you for a while."

Nancy look alarmed. "Is everything okay? Are you getting a divorce?"

"Never," Coen said quickly. "Never. I need her to stay here because I know she'll be safe."

Thatcher glanced at Sydney. "Safe from what?"

Coen turned to Sydney, waiting for her to speak. When she was silent, he continued. "Sydney had a— difficult childhood. She was abused both emotionally and physically. Her stepfather was her tormentor, and her stepbrother was just as worse. Sydney came to Hawaii because she ran away from that past and started a new life. But now that past has followed her. Her mom showed up on our doorstep, asking for refuge from her husband.

"Sydney and I aren't cold. We intend to help her get back on her feet, finding a job and getting her own apartment. Her mother was never there for her, so I'm not too invested in her well-being, but Sydney, with a heart of gold, feels the need to help her. So she's staying at the shack. I'll be there to keep an eye on the place and protect her when Dan shows up. But I don't want Sydney there until her mom is out of the house."

Sydney covered her face, feeling her tears well up.

Thatcher and Nancy were both shocked by the information. Neither one of them spoke.

Nancy came to Sydney and wrapped her arms around her, patting her back gently.

Coen gave them a moment before he kept talking. "Can you please take care of my wife in my stead?"

Thatcher nodded. "I'll protect her with my life."

"He'll never track her down here. Believe me, he isn't bright. I just feel better knowing she isn't around that life anymore. I have to protect her from that."

"I completely understand," Thatcher said. "I have an alarm system so there shouldn't be a problem. And her bedroom can be right next to ours."

"Thank you so much," Coen said. He extended hand and shook Thatcher's.

Nancy pulled away, tears in her eyes. "I had no idea, Syd."

She sniffed. "No one did."

"You're safe with us."

Thatcher stared at her. "I have even more respect for you than I already did. You started a new life for yourself, yet you still have the ability to give your mother grace. It's very admirable."

Sydney nodded. "Thank you."

"You'll love it here," Nancy said. "Make yourself at home."

"As soon as I get her mother out of the house, I'll fetch her," Coen said. "I don't want her to infringe on your hospitality too long."

"Shut up," Nancy said. "Sydney is family. She could live with us forever if she wanted to."

Sydney smiled. "Thank you."

"Well, should we get her belongings?" Thatcher asked.

"Everything is in the truck."

"Let's do it," Thatcher said.

The two men left the house.

Nancy sat across from Sydney. "I had no idea…"

"It wasn't my finest hour…"

"I'm not judging you for it."

"You aren't?" Sydney asked.

"Of course not."

"Thank you."

Nancy patted her hand. "You're my best friend. I love you."

"I love you too," she whispered.

Nancy pulled her hand away and looked down. "My mom left me when I was a year old. Now she's in jail for shoplifting. And my dad is a billionaire but we lost touch for a while because all he cared about was money."

Sydney stared at her, surprise on her face. "Wow…"

"Yeah."

"I had no idea."

"I guess we all have our secrets," Nancy said.

"Apparently," Sydney said with a laugh. "Have you told anyone?"

"Just Thatcher."

Sydney nodded.

The men returned with all of Sydney's bags. They placed them in the spare bedroom.

Sydney looked at Nancy. "Thank you for letting me stay here."

"Please don't thank me," Nancy said. "Family is always welcome here."

Sydney smiled.

"Coen loves you so much," Nancy said. "Do you know how hard it's going to be for him to stay at home with your mom? Who he doesn't even like?"

"He's the most selfless person I know."

"We're both so lucky that we found great guys."

Sydney nodded. "Aaron and Derek were pathetic excuses for boyfriends."

"I like the topic of this conversation," Coen said when he walked back into the room.

Thatcher nodded. "I like it when my lady says flattering things about me."

"I always say flattering things about you," Nancy said.

Thatcher rubbed his nose against hers.

"Syd, I hope you don't mind, but Thatcher and I are still having sex even though you're in the next room," Nancy said.

Sydney laughed. "I don't mind in the least. I want to burden you as little as possible."

"Well, I guess I should go," Coen said. "It's getting late."

Sydney felt her happiness die.

Thatcher turned to Nancy. "Baby, let's go in the office."

"Okay," she said.

They left the room, leaving Sydney and Coen alone.

"Call me if you need anything," he said quietly.

Sydney tried not to cry. "This is so hard…"

"Baby, I know. But it will be okay. I promise."

"I can't sleep without you."

He kissed her forehead.

"And I hate not seeing you."

"You'll still see me. Don't worry about that." She walked with him to the door downstairs. He pulled her into his arms and pressed his face close to hers. "I'll get her out of there as soon as possible so we can be together. I promise."

Sydney sniffed.

"I hate this as much as you do. But I have to put you first."

"I know. I'm sorry. This is all my fault."

"I never want to hear you say that again." His words were full of anger. "Ever."

She stared into his eyes.

Coen grabbed her face and kissed her gently, parting her lips with his. "I love you."

"I love you too."

"Call me when you go to bed."

"Okay."

He kissed her forehead before he left.

Sydney watched him get into his truck and drive away. Even though the separation was temporary, it was brutally painful. It reminded her of the break up they had before they were married. It was the most pain she'd ever been in. Not sleeping with her husband was unbearable. She felt like a piece of her was missing.

She went upstairs and walked into the spare bedroom. It had a bed and dressers for a visitor. She sat on the bed and stared at the wall.

"Should do something with her?" Nancy asked. "Take her out?"

"No," Thatcher whispered. "Just give her space. I'm sure she's in pain right now."

"I could never be apart from you, Thatcher."

"Neither could I."

Sydney changed and got into bed, not wanting dinner. When her eyes grew heavy, she called Coen. "I'm going to bed."

"Okay."

"What are you doing?" she whispered.

"I'm lying on the couch."

"Where's my mom?"

"I gave her the bedroom."

"Oh."

She sighed then moved the phone. "Well, goodnight."

"Don't hang up," he said.

"Okay."

He sighed again. "Stay on the phone with me tonight. That way I can still sleep with you."

Sydney felt the tears fall from her eyes. She sniffed loudly, trying to control them.

"It'll be okay, baby," he whispered. "I'm right here."

"I miss you so much."

"I know. I miss you too."

She controlled her breathing and kept the tears back.

"I'm always with you even if you can't see me."

She positioned the phone on the pillow then lied on top of it.

"Listen to me breathe," he whispered.

She did. Her eyes felt heavy. When she pretended he was next to her, she fell asleep.

13

When Sydney woke up the next morning, Coen was still on the phone.

"Hello?" she said quietly.

"I'm here," he said with a yawn.

"That wasn't so bad."

"We can do that every night," he said.

"I *need* to do that every night."

"I need to get ready for school."

"Okay," she said. "I'll see you soon then."

"I love you, baby."

"I love you too.="

He hung up.

Sydney sat up and sighed. The smell of coffee drifted through the crack of the door and tickled her nostrils. She got ready for the day then walked into the kitchen. Henry stood up when he saw her, a look of pain on his face.

Sydney stared at him but didn't speak, not knowing what to say.

Henry wrapped his arms around her and held her close. "I'm so sorry."

She rested her head on his shoulder. "It's okay."

His hand rubbed her back. "I'm always here if you need to talk."

"I know," she whispered.

He continued to hold her, not intending to release her anytime soon.

Thatcher and Nancy sat at the table, averting their gaze to give them privacy.

Henry took a deep breath. "I love you so much."

She pulled away and looked into his eyes, seeing the redness form. "I love you too."

"I'm so sorry that happened to you."

"I'm okay now," she said gently.

He blinked a few times and controlled his emotion. "Let me know if you need anything."

"I will."

"Let's have some breakfast," he said, taking her hand.

When they sat down at the table, Sydney wasn't hungry. She was too depressed to have an appetite. She ate the food anyway, not wanting to be rude.

"You can stay with me and Ren if you get tired of these two," Henry said.

"Thank you," Sydney said. "But I'm sure I'll be fine."

"Okay," he said.

Her friends talked over breakfast while she ate quietly, not wanting to participate in a conversation. All she thought about was Coen. She hoped he was getting along with her mother.

When she went to school, she kept counting down the hours until she had class with Coen. When their molecular biology class arrived, she waited outside for him. When he came around the corner, she ran and jumped into his arms.

He smiled when he caught her.

"I miss you."

"I miss you too." He kissed her forehead.

"How are you getting along with my mom?"

"We're okay," he said. "I guess I'll always discriminate against her because of your past."

"That isn't fair," she said.

He stared at her incredulously. "I'm not going sweep that under the rug, Sydney. She should have went to jail for that."

"She apologized."

"When?" he snapped. "I don't remember her ever saying those words."

Sydney realized he was right.

"Let's get to class."

They walked inside and took their seats. They never showed affection when they were in class, but Sydney rested her left hand on his thigh, needing to touch him in some way. Coen smiled at her then returned his attention to the board.

When lunchtime came around, they didn't go to the cafeteria.

"Let's go off campus," Coen said as he took her hand.

"Where are we going?" she asked.

"In the back of my truck," he said simply.

They hadn't had sex in a few days, and it was killing both of them. Sydney was going crazy. They got into his truck then parked under the shade of a few trees in the rear of the area.

"This is illegal," she said as she moved in the back.

He followed her. "It doesn't seem like you care."

She pulled up her dress the moved her thong over. "Right now, I don't."

He pulled off his jeans and boxers quickly. "Neither do I." He pulled her hips to him then inserted himself inside her. "Fuck."

She grabbed his ass and pulled him into her. "Coen…"

He thrust hard and fast. "You've never been wetter."

"Fuck me harder."

"Or dirtier," he said between his breaths.

Sydney gripped him as she enjoyed feeling him. The car was shaking and there was no doubt what they were doing. It felt so good. They hadn't had sex in so long. As soon as they began, her body crumbled and orgasm exploded. "Oh…god."

Coen rocked into her hard, her leg over his shoulder. He was breathing deeply, frantically. The sweat was dripping done his chest and to his stomach. His cock was pulsing deeply, bring him to the edge he needed.

"I love it when you fuck me like that."

Coen held on a moment longer and moved into her as fast as he could.

"Right there," she said. "I'm about to cum again."

He rubbed her clitoris, giving her the extra push she needed.

"Yes!" Her nails dug into his ass.

Coen felt the explosion inside him. He pushed as far as he could inside her, releasing. "I love cuming inside you." He moaned loudly, practically yelling.

Sydney's head rolled back as she caught her breath. "That was good."

"That's what happens when you don't have sex for a long time."

"Why don't we fuck more often?"

He grabbed her face and kissed her. "Because I love making love to you."

"Well, I love it to. But that was pretty great."

"Let's incorporate it into our lifestyles more often."

"Deal."

He pulled out of her then dressed himself. "Now let's have lunch."

"They'll know what we were doing."

"Do you think I give a shit?" Coen said. "I know Henry fucks Renee in his car all the time."

"He does?"

He smiled. "Guys talk too."

"Apparently." She moved to the passenger's seat.

"And they all know you love anal."

"I miss you so much that I can't be mad at you."

"I guess this is a good time to mention that big spaghetti stain I left on one of the cushions."

She wrapped her arms around his waist and held him. "I don't care."

He kissed her forehead. "I love you too."

She sighed, sadly. "Any luck on job applications?"

"I left my computer so she could search herself. We'll work on it when I get home."

Coen drove back to the front of the parking lot and they went to the cafeteria. They got their lunches then sat down. Sydney didn't care about her friends at the moment. All she wanted was Coen. Now she had to treasure what little time she had with him. She touched his shoulder and kissed his neck randomly. Coen would grab her face and give her a passionate kiss, disregarding everyone else.

Henry cleared his throat. "How are things going with Syd's mom?"

"I'm trying to find her a job so my wife can move back in," Coen said.

Henry pulled out a folder. "I found these today. I don't know what skills she has, but these are entry level positions."

Sydney smiled at Henry. "You're so sweet."

"I just hate seeing you in pain."

Coen nodded. "Thank you." He opened the folder and skimmed through it. "I think some of these might work."

"I'm glad I could help," Henry said.

"So, why were you guys late?" Derek asked.

"We were fucking in my truck," Coen said simply.

Henry nodded. "Word."

Sydney blushed.

"High-five," Derek said.

Coen smacked his hand.

"Did you do anal?" Derek asked.

Sydney glared at Coen.

Coen smiled. "Not this time."

When they finished lunch, they went their separate ways.

"Can I see you before you leave?" Sydney asked.

"Yeah, I'll meet you at your car," he said.

"Okay."

She went to her classes and tried to concentrate. She wanted the period to move faster, to go by quicker. When her classes were finally done, she practically sprinted to the parking lot. When she landed in his arms, she kissed him passionately, pinning him against the Jeep.

He smiled when he pulled away. "I like your enthusiasm."

"I just love you."

"Keep loving me."

"Can we go in the back of your truck before you head to work?"

"I would love to but we don't have time."

She pouted her lips.

"I'm sorry. I'll slip it in whenever I have time. No pun intended."

She chuckled.

"Call me before you go to bed," he said.

"Okay."

He kissed her forehead. "Have a good day. And call me if you need anything."

"I will."

Coen walked away and got into his truck before he drove away.

Sydney sighed then headed to work. The lab wasn't nearly as exciting now that she and Coen weren't living together. She thought about him constantly, and the depression affected every avenue of her life. Their separation was painful.

When she went to Nancy's, she was just as miserable.

They had dinner together then watched TV on the couch. She noticed Nancy and Thatcher didn't show any affection when they were around her. That made her feel worse.

"You guys don't have to hide your happiness from me," Sydney said. "Don't tone down your affection."

Nancy smiled. "You caught that?"

"I know how affectionate you are," Sydney said with a smile. "You tell me in great detail."

Nancy moved to Thatcher's lap.

When it was late, Sydney went to bed. She called Coen when she was inside the covers.

"Hey," he said quietly. "Going to bed?"

"Yeah."

"Your mom applied to a few jobs. We'll see what happens."

"Do you want to rip her head off yet?"

"She's not that bad, actually," he said.

"I'm glad to hear that."

He sighed.

"Are you lying on the couch?"

"Yeah, your mom is already asleep."

Sydney took a deep breath.

"I'm really horny for you right now," he whispered.

"I'm always horny for you."

"Even right now?"

"Yeah," she said quietly.

"Hold on." He put the phone down then picked it up a minute later. "Touch yourself."

"What?" she asked incredulously.

"I know you know how. I showed you."

"But I like it better when it's you."

"Pretend," he whispered. A faint moan escaped his lips. "That's what I'm doing." He continued to breathe into the phone, his quiet sighs becoming louder. Hearing it was making her hot. She reached down and touched herself.

"Are you doing it?" he said with a sexy voice.

"Yeah…"

"Now pretend it's me."

"Oh…"

Coen continued to breathe into the phone. "You're on all fours on the bed, and I'm fucking you from behind."

"Yeah..."

"You're tight, warm, whispering my name."

"Coen..." The pleasure hit her unexpectantly. She touched herself harder, making it last as long as possible. She moaned loudly, unable to stop herself. She knew Coen was coming at the same time by the sounds he was making.

"Mmm...."

She caught her breath then closed her eyes.

"That was good," he whispered.

She turned on her side and held the phone to her ear.

"Goodnight, baby."

She was already asleep.

14

The next week was just the same. Sydney missed her husband like crazy. Nancy and Thatcher were supportive and gave her everything she needed, but they weren't Coen. It wasn't the same not living with him. A few times, she called Coen and told him she was coming home, but he talked her off the ledge. He understood her frustration because he felt the same way.

Her mom had a few interviews but nothing stuck. Sydney was disappointed every time Coen told her the bad news. Sydney was becoming more and more frustrated every day. It was ridiculous that she couldn't stay in the same house as Coen. Now she hated Dan more than ever.

Coen came over for dinner during the week, but only because Sydney begged him to.

"Thank you for coming," she said as she held him tightly.

"I can only stay for a little while."

She sighed sadly.

"I have to protect your mom. I can't do that if I'm here."

"I know. I just miss you…"

He kissed her forehead. "I miss you too."

Thatcher placed the dinner on the table and they gathered around.

Coen took a bite of the taco. "This is good, Nancy."

Nancy smiled. "Thatcher is the cook around here."

"Really?" he asked.

Thatcher nodded.

"That's badass," Coen said. "I can only make macaroni and cheese."

"If I'm not around to feed him, he starves," Sydney said. "What have you been eating while I've been gone?"

"Your mom cooks for me."

"Oh."

Nancy put down her fork. "Thatcher and I have been talking about the issue with your mom..."

"Oh?" Coen asked.

"Well, Thatcher and I need a secretary. After I was—promoted—we never hired someone to take my place. She could work for us. It comes with good pay and benefits."

Sydney smiled. "That's so sweet."

"It is," Coen said.

"But we can't accept," Sydney said.

"Why not?" Nancy asked.

"My mom...she's different. She's not reliable and you would be working closely with her. I wouldn't want to do that to you."

"Oh," Nancy said.

"I just have to be honest," Sydney said. "You guys are family. The last thing I want is to put you in an uncomfortable situation, one that you're stuck with."

"Thank you for your honesty," Thatcher said.

"Well, she could work at my dad's hotel as a room cleaner. The pay is better than it used to be. She wouldn't be working directly for me or my dad. And you can tell her that she was just picked without any connections. That way she won't slack off."

Sydney nodded. "That's an idea."

"I'm full of them," Nancy said with a smile.

"Are you sure that's okay?" Sydney said. "I don't want to take advantage of you."

"Consider it done. That hotel is going to be mine someday. I call a lot of the shots."

Coen got up and hugged Nancy tightly. "Thank you."

Nancy laughed as she clapped him on the shoulder. "You're welcome."

"I finally get my wife back." He pulled away and returned to his chair. "Now we need to find her an apartment."

"With what money?" Sydney said. "We have to wait until she gets paid."

"Shoot me now," Coen said with a sigh.

"Thatcher and I can take of that," Nancy offered.

"No," Coen said. "Absolutely not. The job is more than enough."

Nancy looked at Sydney. "Then she can stay in my dad's hotel for a few weeks until she gets paid."

"Are you sure?" Sydney asked.

Nancy nodded. "My dad will do pretty much whatever I tell him."

Coen jumped up and hugged her again. "I love you."

Nancy laughed. "I love you too."

Coen returned to Sydney. "I'm so glad to get rid of her. I want to sleep with my wife again. I miss hearing you laugh in your sleep."

"I don't laugh in my sleep," Sydney said.

"You do," Coen said with a smile. "And it's adorable."

Sydney smiled.

"So, you're coming home tomorrow."

"Okay."

"This week has been hell," Coen said.

"I can only imagine," Thatcher said.

"At least your stepdad never came after her," Nancy said. "That's something to be grateful for."

"And he better not," Coen said.

"If he hasn't come yet, I doubt he's going to," Sydney said.

"Maybe."

"So let me come home with you tonight," Sydney said.

Coen looked torn. "Uh…"

"Come on, Coen. Please," Sydney said. "Do I have to beg you?"

"My wife doesn't have to beg for anything."

"Then let me come home." She was practically on the verge of tears. "Please."

"Okay," he said. "Okay."

She wrapped her arms around him and held him tightly. "Thank you."

Coen ran his fingers through her hair gently.

They finished their dinner then helped with the dishes. Sydney packed all of her belongings in a flash then carried the bags to the stairs.

Coen smiled at her. "Excited?"

"You have no idea."

Coen turned to Thatcher and shook his hand. "Thank you for letting Sydney stay here."

"There's no need for gratitude."

Nancy hugged Sydney. "Now go home and have sex with your husband."

"Oh I will."

"Well, you mom is still there…" Coen said.

"I don't care," Sydney snapped. "I'm a married woman. I have needs."

Nancy laughed. "I'm sure she'll love to hear that."

Sydney and Coen drove back to the shack, and Coen carried everything inside. Her mother was already in the bedroom, so they moved to the couch.

Coen lay down and pulled her to his chest. He buried his face in her neck and sighed, happy to have his wife returned to him.

"I don't think so," she said as she crawled on top of him. "We aren't sleeping."

"Baby," he whispered. "Your mom is just down the hall."

She sealed her mouth over his and kissed him deeply. That shut Coen up. She pulled down his boxers then removed her bottoms.

He lay back and stared at her, watching her move over him.

She pointed him at her entrance then slid down.

Coen bit his lip. "You have to be quiet."

Sydney ignored him. She gripped his shoulders and rocked into him hard. She felt his cock harden the longer she moved up and down. Feeling him inside her is what she needed right now, to feel the connection that developed as soon as they met.

"Slow down," he whispered, grabbing her hips. "I'm not going to last long at this rate."

She moved into him slowly, feeling him stretch her repeatedly. She pressed her face close to his and kissed him softly, their lips making soft noises as they pulled apart.

"Damn...you're so sexy when you do this. It's hard not to come."

She pressed her forehead close to his. "I love you, Coen."

He moaned. "Seahorse..." He only used the name in the most tender moments. It was when his heart hurt, when he felt connected to her in the strongest way. She was his mate, his life partner forever, and when he felt that love and adoration pour out, it escaped his lips. "I can't wait to get your pregnant."

"We can pretend you are right now..."

"I'm already struggling..."

She rode him hard, feeling the burn between her legs. "Oh...god."

Coen moaned loudly as he thrust from below, coming deep inside her. "Yeah..."

She collapsed on top of him, catching her breath.

"You are really good at that," he whispered.

"I learned from the best."

He kissed her forehead. "That's what I like to hear."

She moved beside him and cuddled with him. "I'm so glad to be in your arms again. I never want to be apart from you."

"I won't let that happen again," he whispered. "I hope you understand that I was protecting you. You are my number one priority. Even if I don't like it, I have to do the right thing. Always."

"I understand."

Coen pulled her to his chest and gripped her tightly, never wanting to let her go. Now that he had the love of his life back, he wasn't going to let her slip away again.

15

When they were having breakfast the next morning, Sydney talked to her mom.

"We found you a job," she said.

"What is it?" her mom asked.

"A cleaning position for Oahu Resort."

"Oh," she said.

"Is that okay?" Sydney asked. "It pays pretty well."

"I guess." She didn't seem too thrilled about it.

"And the hotel is letting you stay there for free for two weeks until you get paid," Sydney said. "Isn't that exciting?"

"I'm not staying in a hotel," her mother said. "Are you kidding me?"

"Well, you're wearing at your welcome pretty fast," Coen said.

Sydney glared at him. "Mom, what do you want to do?"

"I don't want to clean up after people for a living."

Sydney sighed. "Well, this all I could find."

"I'll keep looking."

Coen tensed. "No, you're taking this job. If you don't like it, apply for something else in the meantime."

Her mother picked at her eggs and averted her gaze.

Coen clenched his fist on the table. "I knew she was here just to mooch off you, Syd."

Sydney looked at him. "Coen!"

"It's true!" he snapped. "She was never planning on working. She just wants to get away from Dan and let us support her. No fucking way!"

Her mother looked offended. "I just don't want to clean toilets. Would you?"

"No," Coen said. "That's why I went to college."

"Don't be rude," Sydney hissed.

"Me?" Coen asked incredulously. "She's the one that's got only one thing on her mind."

Sydney held up her hand and silenced him. "Mom, what do you want to do?"

She shrugged. "I like doing hair."

"Then go to beauty school," Sydney said.

"That costs money," her mother said.

Coen's face turned red. "That's why you get a job and pay for it."

"I'm not going to ask you again!" Sydney said, glaring at him. "Shut up!"

"No, I'm not going to let her take advantage of you."

Sydney turned away from him. "Mom, you are going to take this job. If you want something else, then you find it on your own. You'll be staying at the hotel for two weeks. When you get your first check, you can get your own apartment. If you want to go to beauty school, save your money."

She drank from her coffee then pushed it away. "I said I'm not doing it."

Sydney sighed. "Then what do you want?"

"I want to go to beauty school and concentrate on that."

"Let me guess," Coen said. "You want to live here, rent free, and you want us to pay your tuition?"

Denise didn't meet his gaze.

"Well, that's not going to happen," Coen snapped. "You may as well pack your shit and get out of our house now."

Sydney looked at him. "Coen, please leave the room."

He stared at her incredulously, a fire in his eyes. "Are you fucking kidding me?"

"You aren't helping the situation."

"Why?" he asked. "Because I'm not buying into her plan?"

"Just give us a moment."

Coen grabbed his plate and smashed it against the wall. Both women flinched as the shards rained down. "I'm not putting up with this bullshit, Syd. I mean it." He walked into his bedroom and slammed the door.

Sydney sighed and looked at her mother. "Mom, we can't let you stay here."

"If he hasn't come by now, he isn't going to."

"Even if that's true, Coen and I barely get by on our own. We can't afford to take care of another person. And if we could, we would want to have a baby."

"I thought I was always welcome?""

"You are," Sydney said. "But as a guest, not a roommate."

Her mother fell silent.

"You can't rely on other people to take care of you. Mom, you have to be independent. I know it's hard, but you can do it."

Denise ran her fingers through her hair but said nothing.

"I know we've been through a lot. When I was younger, I was always scared and afraid of what he might do to me." She suddenly realized that her mother never apologized for the way she treated her. It made her sick to her stomach. "But I can't take care of you. It isn't my responsibility."

"So you're just going to let me be homeless? Let me starve?"

"You won't be if you get a job."

"I don't understand why your father left you this house," she snapped. "It should have been mine."

Sydney stilled at her words. She wasn't expecting such a comment. "Well, Dad left it to me so it is mine. There's no argument about that."

"It shouldn't be."

"What are you saying?" Sydney said.

"You wouldn't be able to afford to live here if it weren't for this place."

"I have a scholarship," she said. "I could have lived off that if I wanted to."

"So if you have a bunch of money in your savings account?"

She did but she didn't want her mom to know that. "No."

Her mother eyed her. "I was married to your father. It should have been mine."

"But you were cheating on him," Sydney snapped. "Why should it go to you?"

Her eyes widened. "I did no such thing."

"You can't lie to me," Sydney said. "I'm not five anymore. And you are leaving this house one way or another. Even if I wanted you to stay, Coen obviously doesn't want you here. I can't do something he's so strongly averse to."

"So you let him boss you around?"

"Not at all," Sydney said.

"You're kicking me out, then?"

"No, I got you a job and a place to live. You should be thanking me."

"I gave birth to you. You should be supporting me now."

Sydney wanted to scream. She was stupid for thinking her mom would ever change. "You never apologized to me."

Her eyes clouded with confusion. "What?"

"For the way you treated me. You stood by and let Dan beat me, putting me in the hospital."

"What was I supposed to do?" she snapped. "If I intervened he would have beaten me."

Sydney shook her head. "I can't believe you. You should have protected me at the cost of your own life. That's what parents do!"

Coen marched down the hall and reached the table. "I'm getting really sick of this." He glared at Denise. "Get the fuck out of my house and away from my wife."

Her eyes widened in anger. "*Your house?*"

"Yes, my house," Coen said. "I'm married to her. Half of it is mine. Now get out."

"I'm not going anywhere," she said simply.

Coen took a deep breath. "Baby, please smack her for me."

Sydney gripped her hair in frustration.

"And you're welcome, by the way." Coen stared her down. "That bat I took to the chest for you was pretty painful."

"I didn't get a chance to say something," Denise said.

Coen looked at Sydney. "I'm calling the police if she doesn't leave. And I'm not bluffing. She's only here to use us. We were stupid for ever thinking otherwise."

Sydney looked at her mom. "I'll call the police if I have to, even though I'd rather not. Grab your things and we'll take you to the hotel."

Her mom didn't move.

Sydney pulled her phone out of her pocket and made the call.

"Okay, fine," her mom said. "I'll get my things."

Sydney hung up.

Her mom left the room and went into the bedroom.

Coen paced in the kitchen, his hands on his hips. "How did you come from that? I honestly don't understand."

"I don't either," she whispered.

"I fucking hate her. I mean, I actually hate her as much as your stepdad."

Sydney tried not to cry. Just when she thought her mom had made a serious change, had become the parent she always needed, the truth came out. Her mother never loved her. All she cared about was money and being taken care of. That was the only reason why she came to Sydney.

"Seriously, your mother is a fucking bitch. I can't believe someone would treat their own daughter that way. It's despicable."

Sydney hid her face, feeling the tears bubble.

"I've never wanted to hit a woman more in my life, even Audrey!"

She broke down and the tears fell.

Coen stopped when he heard her. "Baby, I'm so sorry. I was being such a fucking asshole." He kneeled before her and cupped her face. "I'm sorry."

She sniffed. "She never loved me. She never did."

Coen felt his heart ache. There was nothing he could say to make her feel better. Her words were fact. Her mother just proved it.

"I've never been good enough for her. It doesn't matter what I say, it doesn't matter what I do."

"Baby, look at me."

Sydney kept averting her gaze.

"My mom loves you like her own. She really does. They invite you over and forget about me entirely. My entire family thinks you're too good for me. My uncle is obsessed with you, thinks you're a genius. Don't let your mom hurt you like this. It says more about her than it does about you."

"I just want to be loved," she whispered.

"You are," he said. "By me. Your friends. My family. We all love you. You don't need her."

Sydney tried to control her breathing. "It's just not fair."

"I know," he said gently. "It kills me every time I think about it."

"I don't know what I would do without you, Coen."

"You're my seahorse. You never have to worry about it." He pulled her to his chest and kissed her on the forehead. "It's alright, baby."

She moved away and wiped her tears. "I'm sorry for crying."

"Why? I was being insensitive."

"I know you would never hurt me on purpose."

"You can always cry in front of me. Don't ever apologize for it."

Her mother came back into the room, her bags in tow.

"I'll get rid of her," Coen said. "Just stay here."

"Okay," she whispered.

Coen walked away and grabbed her bags. "Let's go."

"Isn't Sydney coming?"

"No," Coen said. "She isn't your daughter anymore."

They left the house, leaving Sydney alone. She listened to the silence for a while, letting it soak into her skin. Her youth was all a waste. It was a time of pain and torture, memories that she would do anything to forget. But the fact that her mother really didn't love her, really didn't care, was enough to cripple her. The only people who ever showed her real love were her friends. Without them, she wouldn't have even understood what the word meant. Then Coen came along, making her understand the meaning of trust. He never let her down and she knew he never would.

Sydney put the dishes away, a few tears escaping every once in a while, and then got ready for the day. Coen wasn't back within an hour and she wondered what was taking so long. He was probably yelling at her mother, making her feel like shit for the way she treated Sydney. Even though Coen was argumentative and stubborn, he defended her in every way. It didn't matter who the attacker was. Coen would rip them apart for ever hurting her. It was like having a human watchdog.

A loud bang against the door made her stiffen. It happened again.

She walked down the hall and headed to front door. Before she looked through the peephole, it thudded again.

"I know you're in there!"

It was Dan.

Sydney felt her heart accelerate. Her first instinct was to grab her phone. She searched for it but couldn't find it because she was so panicked. She looked in her purse but it wasn't there. The counter was spotless. The space between the cushions was empty.

"Open the fucking door!" he yelled.

Sydney cursed to herself. Now she wished she had a land line.

The door cracked as he threw his body against it.

Sydney ran to the closet and grabbed the bat Coen stored in there. She came to the front door and waited.

He finally crashed it down, looking sweaty and hot. When he saw Sydney, he glared at her. "Where's that bitch?"

Sydney wasn't offended by the insult. "She's not here."

"Don't fucking lie to me."

Sydney tightened her grip. "She isn't here. Now get off my property."

Dan looked around. "Where's that watchdog of yours?"

She didn't answer.

"I think you're telling the truth for once." He looked over his shoulder. "Johnny, come in."

Sydney felt her neck sweat. They were both here.

"Looks like your sister is all alone."

"I'm not his sister," she said automatically.

He stared her down. "You're being awfully rude. Is that how you address your father?"

Sydney felt the insult sting. She knew exactly why he said those words. To get a rise out of her. "You aren't my father," she said firmly.

"I was hoping you'd say that." He stepped closer to her, his arms flexed for battle. He glanced at the weapon. "You think I'm scared of that?"

"You should be," she snapped.

"Johnny, hold her down. I'll do the rest."

Sydney didn't like the sound of that.

"I'm sure your husband will be happy," he said with a smile.

"To kill you," she said.

He raised his hands and stepped toward her.

Sydney gripped the bat and held it close to her body.

Dan stepped to the left while Johnny moved to the right.

Sydney remained calm, remembering everything Coen taught her. This was a moment she had been waiting a long time for. And she had a weapon. She would love to bash their faces in.

"Now!"

Dan moved in at the same time as Johnny.

Sydney swung the bat and collided with Dan's side. Johnny took the opportunity to jump on her. Sydney pushed her palm up, hitting him in the nose. He screamed and cowered back. Sydney swung the bat and hit Dan in the shoulder.

He screamed then grabbed her leg, forcing her to the ground.

Sydney rolled out of the way then got to her feet. Johnny came behind her and pushed her to the ground, pinning her down with his large size. Sydney fought his grasp but he held her too tight. She struck her head back, hitting him in the nose again.

"Fucking bitch!" he screamed.

Dan reached for her but she kicked him in the groin, making him moan in pain.

She rolled then grabbed the bat, but Dan kicked it away. He grabbed a fist of her hair then pulled as hard as he could, tearing the strands out. Sydney screamed then fought against him, trying to get away.

"Johnny, grab the bat!"

Johnny ran to it then picked it up.

Dan held her arms to her sides. Sydney tried to head-butt him but he was too tall. She twisted and screamed, trying to get away. Dan dug his fingers into her sides. "Give her a nice hit to the ribs."

Sydney stomped on his shoe and he winced in pain. She tried to get away but he wouldn't let her.

"Hit her! Teach this bitch a lesson!"

Johnny held up the bat, ready to strike.

The door burst open again as Coen smashed it to pieces with his large size. The look on his face was indescribable. His eyes were bigger than Sydney had ever seen them. The look of murder on his face showed everything he intended to do to them. Every muscle was flexed, every tendon was sprung.

Johnny swung the bat at Coen, but Coen grabbed it and broke it in half with his   bare hands. Johnny stepped back, frightened. Coen grabbed both pieces and slammed them against either side of his head. Johnny immediately dropped to the floor, completely out.

Coen rushed Dan next. He punched him in the face then hit him in the neck, making him lose his breath for a moment. Sydney felt his hold loosen so she pulled away. Coen grabbed her and shoved her behind him. She fell to the ground out of harm's way.

Coen grabbed him by the neck and slammed his face into his knee. Sydney moved further away, afraid of Coen's bloodlust. Coen yelled as he slammed Dan's body to the floor. The wooden floorboards shuttered with the amount of force that collided against the foundation. Dan tried to roll away, but Coen grabbed him by the neck, squeezing his windpipe as he dragged him across the floor.

"Nobody touches my wife like that." His eyes were wide with rage. He squeezed his throat.

"I'm sorry," Dan said, his voice coming out as a whisper.

Coen slammed his head against the ground.

Sydney covered her face, shocked by the violence Coen showed.

"What the fuck did you say to me?" Coen snapped.

Dan was barely holding on to consciousness. "I— I'm sorry."

Coen spit on him then punched him in the sternum, making him gasp in pain. "This is the moment when you die."

"Please don't kill me!" Dan started sobbing. "Please don't."

Coen slammed his head again. "Shut the fuck up!" He grabbed his hair and dragged him across the floor. The blood smeared everywhere.

"Coen, don't," Sydney said.

He looked at her. "The reason why you and I fit together so well is because you have compassion, love, empathy, and forgiveness. I have none of these things."

"Coen, please don't do this."

"Please," Dan sobbed. "Don't kill me."

"Nobody fucks with me wife and gets away with it."

"What about Johnny?" Sydney said.

"You think I give a shit?"

"Coen, if you love me, you won't do it."

Coen glared at her, the rage still burning.

"Please," she whispered.

Coen slammed his head against the ground again, knocking him unconscious.

Sydney covered her face.

Coen rushed to her then grabbed her. "Are you okay?"

She nodded, unable to speak.

Without preamble, he pulled her clothes away, searching for injuries.

"They didn't hurt me."

Coen ignored her. He checked her everywhere. When he got to her head, he saw where her hair had been pulled. His stared at it then returned his look to her face. "You're safe. I'm here."

"I know."

He wrapped his arms around her and held her to his chest. He pulled out his phone and called the police.

Sydney sobbed into his chest, finally admitting how scared she was.

When Coen finished the call, he hung up. "We can still kill him."

"No," she said.

"I'll do it. You don't have to."

"No," she whispered.

He sighed in annoyance.

"I love you so much, Coen."

"I love you, baby."

"I was so scared."

"It's over now." He ran his fingers through her hair.

When the police came, they examined the scene and took Dan and Johnny to the hospital. They questioned Sydney and Coen, and they relayed the truth in its entirety. Coen didn't release his hold on her, supporting her the entire time.

After everything was said and done, the police left the shack.

Sydney was still in shock about the attack.

Coen sat beside her on the couch. He was still in survival mode. His eyes were constantly moving and his muscles were still flexed for battle. The cloud of darkness still hung over him. Sydney could feel his need for bloodshed. "Why didn't you call me?" he said calmly.

"I couldn't find my phone," she answered.

He glanced down. "It's in your pocket."

She immediately reached down and felt it, feeling stupid.

"We miss a lot of details when we feel threatened," Coen said.

She leaned her head on his shoulder. "I'm sorry about all of this."

"I told you to never say that again," he snapped.

"Sorry…"

"Why didn't you let me kill them?" he asked. "I shouldn't have fucking listened to you. I should have just done it." He slammed his fist in his chest, the anger escaping his every breath.

"Have you ever killed anyone before?" she whispered.

He looked at her. "No."

"I would never want that hanging over your head."

"Believe me. I wouldn't have felt any remorse."

"You say that now."

He turned away. "Did they hurt you?"

"I already said no."

"I'm just making sure."

She ran her hand up and down his arm. "What happened with my mom?"

"I checked her into the hotel. I told her she can either take the job or be homeless. I don't care what she chooses."

Sydney nodded.

"Were they looking for her?"

"Yes."

"Then why did they attack you?"

"Because they knew you weren't there."

He clenched his fists again.

She grabbed his hand. "Everything worked out. We're okay. You can calm down."

He pulled his hand away. "When I walked through the door, you were being held in place while Johnny prepared to take a swing at you. No, we aren't okay. I'll never be okay. That image will haunt me until the day I die. I'm not going to fucking calm down."

Sydney sighed. "It's over."

"It'll never be over as long as they're alive."

"They won't come back, Coen."

"Why won't they?"

"They are scared of you. You don't know how you look when you get like that."

"Like what?"

"When you go on a psychotic rampage."

"My wife was almost beaten," he said. "Of course I'm going to snap."

Sydney knew nothing she said would calm him down. He was too angry, too upset to be pragmatic. She rubbed her fingers into his back, massaging the muscle. She was silent as she attended to him, hoping her touch would diminish the anger he had.

He suddenly stood up and marched to the front door.

"Where are you going?" she asked.

"I'm just too fucking pissed to be around you right now."

"I didn't do anything."

"I know you didn't," he said. "I hate myself for not killing him." He slammed the door shut.

144

16

Coen was still withdrawn for the following days. Sydney didn't push him to open up. She gave him the space he clearly needed. They slept together every night, but they never made love. He was quiet at lunch and silent in the evenings. Sydney was starting to get worried. He usually got over things within a day or two.

They didn't tell anyone what happened. It was something they silently agreed on. It would just worry everyone. Sydney's mom stayed at the hotel and started working as a room cleaner. She called Sydney a few times, but Sydney didn't answer it. Coen ignored the call before Sydney could even grab the phone.

Their friends noticed the aggressive tone to their relationship but no one commented on it. Nancy asked how Sydney's mother was doing, and Sydney always made up a story. Coen made it clear she could never talk to her mother again, which was fine with her. She wanted nothing to do with her.

Since Coen was so distant, she spent more time in the lab than she normally did. She stayed late and worked on their project, making sure they were always ahead of schedule. Since her husband was so angry, she felt better being somewhere else. Whatever issues he had, he needed to work on them by himself.

When she came home that night, Coen was sitting in the living room. All the lights were out.

She stopped and stared at him. "You are really starting to scare me."

He stood up and approached her. "I'm sorry."

"What's going on with you? You've been this way for a week."

He sighed. "I—I feel like I failed you."

She stared at him incredulously. "Where is this coming from?"

"I didn't protect you."

She shook her head. "That isn't how I remember it."

"You don't get it," he snapped.

"Then explain it to me."

"I should have killed him, both of them."

She ran her fingers through her hair. "I didn't want you to. I would never want you to."

"But it doesn't matter what you want. I should have done what's best for you."

"I wouldn't want to be married to a murderer."

"I'd be doing the world a favor."

She grabbed him by the shoulders. "You did the right thing, Coen. Please stop beating yourself up for it. That couldn't have gone any other way. And they'll be in jail soon."

"Not for long," Coen said. "I'm sure they'll get out."

"So what? They won't bother us anymore."

"There's no guarantee," he said. "We need to move."

She glared at him. "I'm not leaving this house—ever. This is my home."

"I have to protect you."

"Coen, no. I'm not running from him, living in fear. He won't bother us again. Dan knows you could kill him if you really wanted to."

Coen looked away.

"Please drop it," she begged. "Please. I want my husband back. I haven't seen him all week."

"You're right," he said quietly.

She cupped his face and kissed him gently. "Now be happy with me."

"I am happy."

She pressed her face close to his. "Then let's move on."

"Okay."

"I love you, Coen."

"And I you."

"Now make love to me."

He smiled. "You get right down to business."

"I've been horny for days."

"I haven't been a very good husband."

She gave him a serious look. "You've been the best husband ever." She grabbed his hand and dragged him to the bedroom.

After they made love, they lied together in silence.

Coen cuddled next to her, being more affectionate than he had all week. His lips trailed down her skin, planting light kisses everywhere. She lied back and enjoyed it. Her phone rang on the nightstand but she didn't reach for it. Coen kept kissing her. It rang again and Sydney sighed. She glanced at the screen.

"Don't answer that," Coen snapped.

Her mother's name was on the screen.

Sydney didn't touch it.

She called again.

"It must be important," Sydney said.

"You think I care?"

Sydney answered it. "Hello?"

Her mother was crying. "Dan…"

"What happened?" Sydney asked.

"He—he died."

"What? What are you talking about?"

"He had a heart attack this morning."

Sydney didn't know what to say. "Oh."

She sniffed into the phone. "It's just so sudden."

"But isn't this a good thing?"

"My husband died! Of course it isn't a good thing." She continued to cry on the phone.

Sydney couldn't empathize with her. After Dan and Johnny tried to beat her, her mother shouldn't care that Dan was dead. She should be happy, not mournful. That's when Sydney realized that she didn't have a mother. She never had a mother. The only one she had was Vivian, Coen's mom. And that's all she ever needed. "Denise, don't ever call me again." She hung up and returned the phone to the nightstand.

"What was that about?"

"Dan died."

"How?" he asked.

"Heart attack."

"Fuck yeah!" he said happily. "I hope the piece of shit burns in hell."

"I knew you didn't have to kill him," Sydney said.

"And why did you call her Denise?"

"Because she isn't my mom," Sydney said simply. "She was crying about his death even though he tried to hurt me. What kind of person does that?"

Coen stared at her with a sympathetic look.

"She was never my mother. The only person I've ever had is yours. And I'm happy with that."

"She loves you very much."

Sydney nodded. "I've felt more love from them in this short amount of time than I've felt my whole life."

"Because you deserve to be loved—by the right people."

"I've finally let it go."

He smiled. "I can tell."

She hugged him tightly. "You are my family."

"I'm your seahorse," he whispered. "And we'll make our own family someday."

"Well, everyone already thinks I'm pregnant," she said with a laugh.

"It's just wishful thinking."

"When do you want to have them?" she asked.

He leaned down and kissed her stomach. "When we have money."

She laughed. "We'll never have money, especially as researchers."

"We better start growing our own food, then," he said with a laugh.

"I want to have the first one in a couple of years."

He kissed her forehead. "Whatever you want."

"And I want to have a boy and a girl."

"And another girl," he said.

"You want three?"

He nodded.

"Just like your parents?"

"Yeah."

"Well, we need to keep practicing."

"I do need to work on a few things," he said as he rubbed his nose against hers.

"I beg to differ."

17

"What are your plans for spring break?" Henry asked.

Sydney picked at her fruit. "Nothing. Coen and I will probably just be lying around the house."

"You mean, you'll be having sex all week," Ren said with a smile.

"We do that anyway," Sydney said.

"We take our sex lives very seriously," Coen said.

"You always have to be on top of your game," Henry said.

"Literally," Coen said with a laugh.

Sydney sighed. "I wish we were doing something fun."

"Let's go hiking," Coen said.

"That does sound adventurous," Sydney said.

"We can sleep on the mountain," Coen said.

"No," she said. "I like sleeping in a bed too much."

He smiled. "And we can do other things too."

"Yeah," she said.

They finished their classes for the rest of the day then went home to shack. Sydney was relieved to have a week off. She was getting sick of homework, lab reports, and waking up early for school. It would be nice to lay around with Coen.

Ever since Dan passed away, Coen had been in a much better mood. He acted like he was on a very potent strain of Prozac. Sydney didn't mind his delight. And she didn't care that her stepfather was dead. It was a blessing to her. Her mom was obviously upset, but Sydney decided to let it go and forget about it.

Coen came home a few hours later.

"How was work?" she asked.

"It was good. Casey is still diligent in her training."

"Jeremy hasn't bothered her?"

"Nope," he said.

"That's good."

"What do you want to do tonight?" he asked.

"I don't know," she said with a sigh. "We can watch a movie and order a pizza."

"That's funny you said that." He opened his backpack and handed her a DVD.

"You got *The Count of Monte Cristo*?" she asked happily.

"I saw it on sale and I know it's your favorite movie."

"Thank you," she said with a smile. She tore off the plastic and opened it. An envelope fell out. "What's this?"

He shrugged. "Open it."

Sydney eyed him suspiciously before he opened the fold. She stared at it for a long time. "Australia?"

He sat down beside her and took her hand. "I know it's your greatest dream to see the Great Barrier Reef."

She covered her face and dropped the envelope. "Are you fucking kidding me?"

He smiled, happy to see the delight on her face. "No. I'm taking you on a real honeymoon. We would have gone before but I hadn't saved enough money at the same time."

Tears were in her eyes. "Oh my god."

"And I didn't need to buy a wedding ring so I really don't have an excuse."

She wiped her eyes and jumped into his arms. "I can't believe this."

"I'd do anything for you, baby. Just seeing that smile makes it all worth it."

"I've wanted to go since I was a little girl."

"I know," he said. "You've told me many times."

"You have no idea how much this means to me."

"But I do." He rubbed his nose against hers.

"I just can't believe this is really happening. I need to pack!" She jumped off his lap then ran into the bedroom.

He laughed then followed her, watching her shove everything into suitcases.

"When are we leaving?"

"Tomorrow," he answered.

"I need to move fast," she said. "Does everyone know?"

He nodded. "They helped me plan the details, like the flight and the hotel. And the boat arrangements. And Nancy and Thatcher insisted on getting us a honeymoon suite at a renowned hotel. I kept saying no but they wouldn't accept it. So now I have some extra money to take you out."

"That's so sweet."

"Henry paid for a breakfast one morning," Coen said. "I told him but he insisted. And Derek and Paola gave us their free passes to a few museums, not that we'll use them."

"I can't believe they did that…"

"They want to make sure this honeymoon is everything you deserve."

"Coen, we already had our honeymoon. Every day is our honeymoon."

"But now you get a real one."

She hugged him. "You're the best husband in the world."

"I must be doing something right, then."

"You do everything right."

He rubbed his nose against hers. "Because you're my seahorse. We're stuck together for life. It's my job to make you happy."

"No, it's our job to make each other happy."

The story
continues....

Lying in the Sand

(Book Seven of the Hawaiian Series)
Cheyenne and Bryce

Available Soon

About the Author

E. L. Todd was raised in California where she attended California State University, Stanislaus and received her bachelor's degree in biological sciences, then continued onto her master's degree in education. While she considers science to be interesting, her true passion is writing. She is also the author of the *Soul Saga Trilogy, The Alpha Series, and her bestselling novel, Only For You, the first installment of the Forever and Always Series.* She is also an assistant editor at Final-Edits.com.

By E. L. Todd

Soul Catcher
(Book One of the Soul Saga)
Soul Binder
(Book Two of the Soul Saga)
Soul Relenter
(Book Three of the Soul Saga)
Only For You
(Book One of the Forever and Always Series)
Forever and Always
(Book Two of the Forever and Always Series)
Edge of Love
(Book Three of the Forever and Always Series)
Force of Love
(Book Four in the Forever and Always Series)
Fight for Love
(Book Five in the Forever and Always Series)
Lover's Roulette
(Book Six in the Forever and Always Series)
Happily Ever After
(Book Seven of the Forever and Always Series)
Sadie
(Book One of the Alpha Series
Elisa

CPSIA information can be obtained at www.ICGtesting.com
Printed in the USA
LVOW13s1458140814

399159LV00020B/1084/P